# Nice One,

# SNIFF

## Ian Whybrow

Illustrated by

## Tony Ross

Hodder
Children's
Books

a division of Hodder Headline plc

Text Copyright @ Ian Whybrow 1994
Illustrations Copyright @ Tony Ross 1999

First published 1994
by The Bodley Head Children's Books

This edition first published 1998
by Hodder Children's Books
A Division of Hodder Headline plc
338 Euston Road
London NW1 3BH

A catalogue record for this book is available from
the British Library

ISBN 0 340 72261 4

Printed and bound in Great Britain

# Contents

**1** Nice One, Sniff 5

**2** Sniff and Sal's Invisible Friend 31

**3** Sniff Gets Stagestruck 48

**4** Sniff Makes You Wonder 74

**5** Snif and the Laptop 95

**6** Sniff the Hamburglar 109

**7** Snapping with Sniff 132

**8** Sniff and the Binbag 148

**9** Sniff and the Fair Cops 171

**10** Sniff and the Kissmus Present 187

# Nice One, Sniff

My little sister Sal was breastfeeding the ichthyosaurus in the garden. I didn't realize at first, thinking she was just smearing a bit of mud on her chest with it, which is the kind of little kiddie thing she usually does. Then I noticed the way she was talking. She was going, 'Like it? 'Snice. Want some more? Num num.'

I tried to ignore her and get on with walking my stick insect. I like to give him a bit of a run in the hedge now and then, seeing as he likes privet. I'd made him this dead good lead ... more like a harness, really ... out of a load of rubber bands joined together. Now he was having a great time, in a stick-insecty sort of way, doing press-ups, filling his face with leaves, and squirting little green balls out the back.

Sal stopped feeding her ichthyosaurus. Well, it was mine actually, but I let her borrow it. It was supposed to be authentic and modelled to scale and all that, but it had never really looked right since Sniff chewed its legs off.

Sniff. He's our dog - if you can call him ours. We don't exactly own him - he's not that sort of dog, but he hangs out with us, put it that way. He just sort of turned up in the park one day when I'd got lumbered with the job of looking after my little sister.

Sal is one of the screamiest two-and-a-half-year-olds in the known universe and was being a pain as usual. We'd done the swings and the see-saw and everything. I'd even bought her a '99' with sprinkle-spronkle – which kept her quiet while she was licking it and smearing it all over herself. Then she started screaming again, so I stuck her in the sandpit, thinking maybe it would cheer her up a bit if she had something to chuck at the other little kids.

It worked pretty well – except that, what with all that ice-cream on her face for the sand to stick to, she finished up looking like The Thing from the Mummy's Tomb and that scared the daylights out of all her little play-mates. So they all started screaming, which brought their mothers running. Well sad for me, that was – me being supposed to be The Responsible Big Brother and all that. I really thought I was dead, and then suddenly . . .

You guessed it, the 'suddenly' was this great big hairy quadruped, the craziest-look-ing dog you've ever seen in your life! One minute, he was just a loud panting and a pounding of paws. Next minute he was in the sandpit whipping the sand up into a blinding tornado, whizzing round and round and Rrrraaalph-ing his head off. When he saw little Sal lying there like a sheet of 3-dimen-sional sandpaper, he went straight over to her and, with one wet windscreen-wiper SCHLOPPP!, he licked her face clean. Sal thought that was wicked and started laughing and giggling like mad. But all the mums were dead worried, and shouted and waved their arms, trying to get him to buzz off. The poor dozy old bathmat got so embarrassed, he turned round three times and did a poo-poo.

You would have thought he'd done an unexploded bomb, the way all the mums started acting, dragging their weeny ones out of the way before the germs zoomed up and zapped them. Which was lucky because, in the confusion, I managed to get Sal into her pushchair. I was heading for the park gate before they remembered they were supposed to be having a go at us for being antisocial and irresponsible, etc.

Maybe that's what the dog liked about us, or maybe he just liked the taste of Sal, because he was quite happy to trot home with us, occasionally giving her a good sniff and a lick, with her hanging on to him by the hair on the back of his head.

He wasn't wearing a collar or anything, so

we've never found out where he came from, who he belonged to, or what he was called or anything. We advertised to say that we'd found him, but so far nobody's come to claim him. Dad says he's not surprised.

Sal had the idea for his name. When we first got him home, I remember Mum going all red, because he was giving her a good sniffing all over. 'He like you. He miffin,' Sal explained to her. 'He go miff, miff! Dat his name – Miff.' When Dad asked how she knew his name was Sniff, she yelled, 'It is Miff! He telled me!'

He also 'telled' her that he lived with us, apparently, so that was that. Sniff's been part of the Moore family ever since. And the day I'm talking about, weeks later, he'd gone for a wander round somewhere, and me and Sal were up the garden – me for the serious reason that stick insects need exercising, and Sal just so she could play little kiddie games with my ichthyosaurus. I watched her scrape out a hollow in the flowerbed, lay the 'saurus gently in it, say, 'Nigh nigh dallin. Go sleep,' and stamp on it.

I said to her, 'That is sick, Sal. You're supposed to be a nice mummy.' Waste of time. All she did was say 'Shaddup wee-wee boy' and started breastfeeding a guard's van. And it wasn't just any old guard's van. It was the one from Dad's Hornby Double-O set that he keeps in the cupboard under the bookcase in the sitting-room. He's kept the box and everything. I said to her, 'Sal! Dad'll go mad if he finds out you've nicked that!' but I could see it was no good me trying to get it off her, not when she might crack me one with her spade, so I let her get on with it.

I had to concentrate on the stick insect for a while, because he'd got his lead tangled round his mandibles. Next thing I knew, Sal had crawled right over to the shed, knocked over my flowerpot with the slate on top, the one I keep my experimental snails in, and grabbed my best snail.

I yelled, 'Mum! She's got my best snail! Stop her!'

Mum was in the house, doing an aerobic

work-out with her chum from her university days, Atlanta Pitt-Gladwin, who was staying with us for a while. She's this big wobbly woman, dead brainy and fit and everything. Mum tried to explain to me and Dad about how important it is that some women dedicate their life to Art, Shakespeare and Surfing instead of husbands and children. Me and Dad were dead worried in case Atlanta started having a bad influence on Mum, 'specially after she kept Mum up till three o'clock in the morning reading from her latest book of poems called Go Boadicea! and warning her against fried foods. That was one of the reasons why Dad kept shooting off to the garage and re-arranging his tools on their little racks on the wall.

I yelled again. 'Mum, quick, stop Sal! I can't leave my stick insect!' but she ignored me as usual. So I had to tie the lead to a twig and go over there myself and sort her out. When I say go over there myself, I didn't actually get right over there because, as soon as I tied up the stick insect and started moving in Sal's direction, she let rip with this mega scream. She managed to make it sound like some-body was sawing a lump off her with a breadknife. So, BLAM! – the back door crashed open and suddenly there were Mum and Atlanta. Mum was wearing her striped leotard (so embarrassing) and Atlanta was wearing a ginormous black all-in-one down-to-the-ankles lycra body suit. They looked a bit like two of the crew of Starship Enterprise, just after they've got beamed down among the Klingons. They raced each other to the shed while I stood frozen to the lawn. Mum was first to get to Sal – maternal instinct and all that.

Sal rolled herself into a ball and tucked her hands in the middle somewhere, like she does when she has something and doesn't want anybody to take it away from her. 'What is it?' said Mum, meaning which part of you has Ben sawn off, while trying to unroll her like a hedgehog.

'Dat my nail!' Sal lied, going into an even tighter ball. Even from where I was standing,

I could hear the crunch. That set Sal off again like a car alarm.

'Now look what you've let her do!' I said. 'She's killed it!'

'Killed what? Show me. Show Mummy,' Mum begged, all of a dither.

'He bleedin!' sobbed Sal, bringing her fist out and holding it up.

'What's bleeding, darling?' gasped Mum.

'Da nail!' yelled Sal.

'Nail!' squeaked Mum. 'Oh my goodness,

she's stuck a nail in herself. It could be rusty or anything. Quickly, darling. Open your hand and show Mummy.'

Sal had about half a second to show Mum a handful of crunched shell and green slime before . . . Crash! something smacked through the back fence! KERUCKA KADUCKA big hairy feet pounded across the lawn! HUFF-HUFF – there was Sniff with his tongue sticking out and SSSCHLOOP! . . . no green slime.

My turn to start yelling. 'She's destroyed it! She's squashed one of my best snails! She knew I was studying them for a class talk on hermaphrodites! God, I can't even keep worms without her interfering and eating them all the time.'

'What is that dreadful smell?' said Atlanta, ignoring me. Her eyes were practically popping out and her nose was twitching like a rabbit's.

'I have a horrible suspicion that Sniff's been chasing Mr Jenkins' muckspreader again,' said Mum. 'I'm so sorry ...' She clapped her hands at him to make him buzz off down wind a bit.

'How revolting!' groaned Atlanta.

'What about my snail, Mum?' I said, in case she'd forgotten.

'Oh . . . um,' said Mum.

'Be assertive,' advised Atlanta. 'Ben must understand that there are more important issues here. That dog needs disinfecting for a start and . . . look, leave this to me, in fact. I think I can handle this.' She turned to me and said, 'Ben, face it, the snail's dead. Mourn it and move on. Right? Now I'm going to speak my mind to your sister.'

She bent over to get her face level with Sal's. It was the only part of her body that wasn't covered in black lycra so, boy, did it look boiled! It scared Sal stiff.

If Atlanta hadn't looked quite so much like some sort of mega black beachball or inner tube from behind, maybe Sniff wouldn't have come bouncing over and tried to ping her up in the air with his nose. And if she hadn't suddenly felt a cold nose pinging her up the

bott, maybe she wouldn't have let out a yell like the New Zealand Rugby team. And if she hadn't yelled, maybe she wouldn't have freaked Sal out. But that's what happened – so ... screamy time again!

'. . . and Point Number Three,' said Atlanta, looking a touch cooler after a cold shower, and ticking Point Number Three off in her notebook with her silver propelling pencil, 'is that Sal was attempting to – ahem – breastfeed a snail.'

'I told you she was nuts,' I said, and Mum told me to shut up. Sal was being calmed down. In other words, she was sitting in her high chair in the kitchen, being spoiled rotten with Ribena and banana bread. She opened her mouth to shout at me and something brown and chewed slid down her pelican bib.

'She knows about breastfeeding from a video that Robert's cousin sent from Australia to show us their new baby,' explained Mum.

'And you permitted her to watch it!' asked Atlanta. 'My goodness, Jojo, what if you and I had watched that sort of thing as youngsters? A girl of two-and-a-half should be protected from the idea that women are only here to be mothers and food-providers! Where would I be today with my quest for truth if I was tied down with a husband and a couple of sprogs? No, Jojo, that video might have warped Sal's young mind.'

'Well, I don't really think so ...' said Mum, going red.

'Nor do I,' I said. 'It was warped well before that.' I was really cheesed off. 'And I hope you've made a note about her dooming my stick insect as well. She made me forget about it, and now it's got lost in the hedge.' Just as I said 'hedge', Sal scooped a handful of brown gunge out of the bottom of her pelican bib and called 'Miff!' Sniff had been made to stay outside on the patio because of him ponging so much from the muck that had been spread on him, but he must have suspected that there was some grub on offer, because he dived in through the open window. He knocked over a milk bottle and two saucepans that were drying on the draining board and then barged Atlanta out of the way so he could get a good licking at anything that was sticking to Sal. It took me ages to get hold of him and drag him outside again but, in spite of all his whining and huffing, I still managed to hear what Atlanta was saying to Mum: 'Sorry, Jojo, but this is building into a worrying picture. That dog is completely out of control and

the children are running rings round you.
Now I think you'd be wise to allow me to
take them in hand this afternoon. What your
children need is more exposure to culture,
and for an adult to assert herself. Now,
when did you last take them to an art
gallery?'

'Well, not for a while ... but, er ... Sal's little friend Tom's coming over this afternoon,'
Mum said, doubtfully.

'Then I shall jolly well take him as well,'
said Atlanta.

I couldn't see the point of suffering alone, so
I rang up Thurston. 'Fancy coming up to
London this afternoon?' I said.

'What for?' he said. He's such a suspicious
four-eyed little swot. Why I let him be my
best mate, I'll never know.

'My mum's friend's taking me and Sal and
Tom for a treat,' I said.

'Will there be any eating?' he said.

'I wouldn't swear to it,' I said. 'But there
might be ... after a little bit of cultural stuff.

We're sort of looking in on an art gallery first. Just your scene, eh?'

'Pardon my pandiculation,' said Thurston. He paused to check whether I was going to ask him what it meant, but I wasn't going to let him ping me up like that. So he carried on. 'As you know, I'm more than keen on art. But the thought of trailing round some stuffy gallery with you, your mum's friend and a couple of emunctious infants is my idea of hell. So all in all, I think I'll choose to go paintballing. You heard me, Ben . . . paintballing! – proper splatty spatt-splatt – none of your tame old laser stuff. Sorry you can't join me and Max and Bruno. You were invited of course, but . . . tough luck, eh? Splat for now. Enjoy the pictures . . .' And he put the phone down.

I told Mum about going paintballing but she said it was a terribly unhealthy pastime that encouraged the worst kind of male attitudes. 'And besides,' she whispered, 'It'll do Atlanta good to have to look after some children for once, so do me a favour and don't sulk.' Something told me that Mum was getting a bit cheesed off with being reminded she had failed as a mother.

It's annoying to have to admit that Thurston is right about anything, but he was right about that afternoon being hell. Don't ask me what gallery it was. All I know is that somebody should be shot, the things they had on the walls. I've seen better stuff scratched on the inside of Rajan Gudkha's locker. And all the time, there was Atlanta going:

'And here we have a fine example of the work of William Blake, poet, mystic and remarkable illustrator. Who else but this original could have captured the essence of the ghost of a flea? And who but he . . . blahdee blah-blah . . .'

She had miles of that stuff all coiled up inside her head like elastic in a golf ball and it looked as if there was going to be no stopping her. She was going on and on. There's something about art galleries – maybe it's the heat, the smell, the whispering – maybe it's because you wouldn't think there were that many pictures in the whole world – but it makes you go all limp and dozy, even in the first room, and some of these places have billions of rooms. By the third room, I was boiled, brain-dead and starving, and there was Atlanta, striding about in her riding mac, saying 'Who needs Coca-Cola and ice-cream when we have here such a feast for the mind? What shall we gaze at next – the Armenian Impressionists or the Cuboids? You choose, Ben! Come on, boy, we've only got three hours!'

I needn't have worried too much about her keeping it up, though, not with Sal and little Tom around. They were having an ace time, swinging round her legs, giving her their coats and pullies to hold, cooling their tongues on the glass of display cases, having sliding races on the polished floor, and getting warned by grumpy old keepers in black uniforms not to duck under the rope barriers. It was only a matter of time before they started to get to her.

At last we got away from all the paintings and drawings and we came to the sculptures. I couldn't believe it. They had one bloke who had turned a washing machine inside out. Somebody else had done this plaster banana coming out of a toaster, and called it A Leading Question. I would have liked just to ignore it, but I made the mistake of going 'Tuh', really quietly, just to myself. So guess what ... Atlanta started explaining to me. I'm not kidding. She started telling me all her inner thoughts and feelings about it – really, really loud, so that everybody could hear. If Sal hadn't wet her knickers, I would probably still be there having to listen.

I didn't see why I had to carry them, even if they were in a plastic bag, but Atlanta made me, while she took Tom to the ladies because Sal had got him going. She came out looking really pink and fed up. 'Next time he wants to go, you can take him!' she snapped. I guessed what had happened. She hadn't realized you have to point little boys, and he'd peed all over the wall. A lot of people might have given up trying to improve our minds after that, but not Atlanta. We had to move on into another room with sculptures. The one good thing about this room was that she didn't have to explain everything – because it was obvious what everything was: a load of statues with nothing on. Atlanta looked a bit sort of doubtful and she said, 'Keep moving, everyone. More interesting exhibits further on, I think.'

Sal and little Tom were far too interested by the ladies with no knickers on to move further along. 'Look, Tom,' she said, pointing at a statue labelled 'Seated Nude'. 'Da lady sittin on da potty. Assa good lady. Not wee-wee on da floor.'

'Er . . . mustn't touch,' spluttered Atlanta, and would have moved us on if, at that moment, a party of blind people hadn't been led in. Sal and Tom were dead interested, listening to the man explaining things, and watching all the blind people running their hands over the statues. Atlanta was just pointing out to me that it was so thoughtful of the gallery to offer this splendid service, when she noticed that Sal and Tom had their eyes tight closed and were stretching up on their tippy toes, running their fingers over a Greek javelin-thrower's figleaf.

When we got home later that day, Atlanta was looking totally shattered. She suddenly remembered some urgent things she had to do back at her flat . . . and left. We haven't heard from her since.

Wow, did Mum have a go at us! She told Dad that he was a stinker, skiving off somewhere and not sticking around to entertain Atlanta, and that he could jolly well organize a bath for Sniff who was another stinker in more ways than one, and had driven her best friend away by being so smelly and rough.

'And you can help your father, Ben,' she said to me. 'You were just as bad. You were grizzly and ungracious to Atlanta the whole time she was here. And when you've given the dog a good scrub, you can both flipping well take him for a very long walk and dry him off!'

'What about Sal, giving her such a hard time at the art gallery?' I muttered. 'How come you don't blame her and little Tom?'

Mum burst out laughing. 'Oh, all right, I was only kidding!' she said. 'I thought you were all brilliant, really. I'd forgotten what a dreadful pain that woman can be. Didn't do her much good being . . .' (she did Atlanta's booming voice) '. . . assertive, did it? Not with you lot!'

'Dead right!' grinned Dad. 'And it was a total waste of time exposing you lot to culture! Blimey, I wish I'd been there to see her face when Sal and Tom started feeling that javelin-thrower's . . .'

'Yes, all right, that'll do!' laughed Mum. 'Now buzz off, you guys, while I rustle up a celebration supper. Anything you fancy?'

'Anything, so long as it's fried,' I said.

'And plenty of it,' added Dad.

It felt a bit weird, half an hour later, with the

sun quite low in the sky, heading for The Pits in Foxley Wood with Sniff and Dad. The Pits were these deep old claypits, great for BMXing – or even skateboarding if it's really hard and dry – great for war-games too, or for just mucking about with a dog that likes chasing around in the trees and finding you hiding under bushes. I'd been there with Sniff loads of times, usually when I was mucking about with Thurston, Bruno, Max and that lot, but never with Dad. So how come Dad had suggested that we took Sniff there? OK, to dry Sniff off after his bath. But why had he insisted on wearing his overalls? And why had he sneaked two boxes of eggs out of the fridge.

Dad kept giggling as he strode along, laughing to himself and muttering, 'God, I wish I'd been there!' and '. . . love to have seen her face!'

Sniff was drying off nicely, zigzagging along ahead of us, sort of whinnying with excitement and panting and peeing on parked cars, garden gnomes, doorsteps, litter bins, etc. – wherever he felt like. He barked at a couple of cyclists, ran off when he was called to heel, ate a wasp and generally had a wicked time in the late evening sunshine. Even after the bath and the medicated shampoo and everything, even 30 metres away, he still smelled of farmyard. I mentioned this to Dad.

'That's partly what gave me the idea, old Sniffer chasing that muck spreader. You know how he loves getting pelted with anything smelly . . .'

'What idea?' I panted, having to run to keep up with Dad. We were at the edge of Foxley Wood now, picking up the path under the big beeches that leads to The Pits.

'And the other thing was, I hear you missed out on paintballing with Thurston. Bit hard, that and . . . well . . . I've always rather fancied a go at paintballing myself. Not that your mother approves, mind you – nasty male attitudes and all that. So, now that Ms Pitt-Gladwin is out of the way and we are at the perfect spot for a quick paintballing practice ... what say we give it a go? Here's your ammo. You've got twenty-five seconds to take cover.' He handed me a box of eggs.

He went 'Geronimo!', and dashed off into the nearest pit before I had time to get my head together. Sniff went after him, smacking through the bushes and barking with excitement, slithering about. Dad was scrambling up the last few feet of the steep slope on the other side of the second pit. He was just about to heave himself out and take cover in the next pit, when Sniff went charging up behind him, barking his head off and getting in his way. All of a sudden, he blundered into Dad's legs and sent him flying.

'Nice one, Sniff!' I yelled. I grabbed an egg out of my box and chucked it as hard as I could. It went up and up, turning over slowly as it flew. Dad was fifty metres away at least, I swear, lying flat on his face with Sniff sitting just near him, looking interested, as if he was hoping Dad would get up and fall over again. For a second, it was so quiet it was sort of spooky, and then – KERRUNCH! – the beautiful satisfying sound of an egg disintegrating on the back of somebody's head.

So brilliant, the way it feels when your arm just comes over, and most times it would be a thousand-to-one shot, with the target miles away, but this time you let go and you just know there's no way you're going to miss.

I knelt down, right where I was, screaming and yelling Yesss! Yesss! and Sniff was barking and darting in close to sniff at the runny yellow squidge running down Dad's neck. And I could hear Dad laughing his head off and threatening to kill me and telling me to 'Just wait!' Wow! I tell you, that was better than paintballing, better than anything. Wicked!

I remember saying to myself that this was one of those moments that I was going to remember for the rest of my life. Which is when I shouted it out again – 'Nice one, Sniff!' – not for anybody else in the woods to hear, but just because I was wanting to share it with the best Dad and the best, doziest dog in the world.

# Sniff and Sal's Invisible Friend

Normally, if somebody comes up to you while you're on your Nintendo and just stands there, and they've got red, white and blue eyebrows, you just say 'Nice eyebrows' or something like that, and they go away happy.

Not my little sister Sal.

You never really know where you are with Sal. Like that time it turned out I'd sat down on Zigzig – her invisible friend. How was I supposed to know he was watching Mork and Mindy? I'd just come into the room and Sal was on the floor with her back to the telly, wearing her nurse's outfit, pulling the eyelashes off her Rosebud sleepy-doll Aunt

Julia sent her for Christmas. That's Sal's idea of being a nurse. So I thought she wouldn't notice if I changed channels. I sat down on the sofa with the zapper and started flipping. Sal didn't say anything – I thought she'd just crawled off somewhere. Next thing I know, she's behind me going 'Nanoo Nanoo' and whacking me round the ear with her first aid box. I can still feel the dent.

Waste of time telling Mum, too. All she says is how important it is to see things from little children's point-of-view and how insecure they feel. INSECURE? I'll tell you what insecure is. Insecure is about six o'clock in the morning. You wake up and you can smell this really sharp smell, like ammonia. And you open your eyes just a peep and you see a white shape floating just above your face. And you try to move your arms so you can protect your face but you can't – it's like there's a weight on them. Because your little sister is trying to keep her balance and climb over you and steal your Easter egg off your bookshelf at the same time. Her legs are too short to climb over you without touching, so she is standing on your arms. And gradually you realize that the white shape is a steaming great wet nappy. And there is nothing you can do about it. It is only a matter of time before – wobble, wobble – SCHHLUUUMP – right in your face! That is what I call insecure.

Anyway, there were these red, white and blue eyebrows right in front of me in the sitting room, and I'm busy with Sonic the Hedgehog so, as I say, I said 'Cool, Sal' and left it at that, like you do if she's not actually screaming her head off.

Big mistake. She was screaming, but I did-
n't really notice because I had my Walkman
on, playing something loud – Megadeth or
Alice Cooper, I think it was – one of Dad's,
anyway. So next thing I know, she sticks out
her finger and turns the volume up full then
sinks her teeth deep into my arm, just to get
the point home. YEEEEECH! I practically hit
the ceiling. Plus I nearly strangled myself
with the wire, trying to rip the earphones off
in a hurry. I swear I ricked something in my
ear because I had this ringing for yonks afterwards.

Anyway, Sal just stood there while I was in
agony, going on and on about something.
And when the ringing died down a bit, it
turned out she was saying, 'Zigzig told me
sumfink.'

'Oh yeah?' Any normal person could have
seen I was concentrating on something dead
important – trying to capture a few more air
bubbles for Sonic, so I could move him along
this passage with loads of spikes sticking out
– but Sal had to come and tell me about

Zigzig. So even though I knew Zigzig was going to say some stupid little kiddy thing, I had to ask. 'What did Zigzig say?'

'Zigzig bleeded Tom wiv his teef.'

Tom? Sal's little friend Tom? I'd forgotten about him. He'd come over to play while his mum (Bunty, Mum's friend) was helping Mum to insulate the loft or something like that. All I know is that for weeks, every time we went out in the car, we had to go round by B & Q, so Mum could cram in a load of those mega orange rolls of fibre glass stuff. Just because they were on special offer. Dead embarrassing, going around like a plumber or something. Most parents would have stuff like that delivered.

'Come on, Sal!' I said, trying to be reasonable. 'You know Zigzig's invisible. How could he bleed anybody?' Bleep bleep. Sonic started smacking into spikes like crazy. So annoying. I was beginning to wonder whether the megadrive was on the blink.

Sal got hold of my cheek, so her thumb was just in the corner of my mouth and pulled. 'Yowch!' I shrieked. She was digging her nails right in.

'Tum on!' She started dragging me towards the door by my face.

'Where are we going?' I said, trying to humour her.

'Da baffroon! Just listen wot I tell you!' she screamed.

'I'm listening, I'm listening!' I said. We were halfway up the stairs and I finally managed to get her claws out of my cheek. 'But why didn't you tell Mummy?'

'I TELLED MUMMY BUT SHE HIDING!'

Mum hiding? She's in a world of her own, this kid, I was saying to myself. There was this thumping noise – CLUMP CLUMP CLUMP – but for the moment I put it down to ear-damage.

When we reached the bathroom, the door was closed. The clumping noise was coming from in there somewhere, but it wasn't quite so noisy as the sound of claws trying to rip their way through one of the door panels. I turned the handle and shoved. I had to push hard but when I finally got the door open out charged Sniff with his tail between his legs, whining, dripping wet and looking like a load of washing that hadn't been properly rinsed or spun dry.

I knew what was going to happen next but what could I do? Some dogs, you can probably say 'Wait, boy. I'll get your towel' and they wait. But, as Dad says, when God made Sniff, he forgot to give him a pause button. So starting with his head and working his way down to the end of his tail, he went into his earthquake routine. In two seconds, I was soaked, Sal was soaked, the carpet was soaked and there were soapsuds all over the landing walls and ceiling. In three seconds, Sniff was down the stairs and under the kitchen table – all innocence – saying to him-self, 'Ha, ha! They'll think I was here all the time!'

Our bathroom is not the tidiest place in the world, but I did think it was a bit strange that there was a ladder in the bath, as well as some weird-coloured water. Later, I worked out how you get that colour. You run the bath and, while it's running, you empty everything you can find into it – shampoo, conditioner, baby-oil, bath essence, Jiff, hard-skin remover, Nivea, suntan oil, shaving-cream, after-shave, Dettol, toothpaste – all stuff like that. And then you stir it round in the bath with the lavatory brush. Which is what Sal and Tom had been doing. They were also responsible for:

1    The artwork in toothpaste on the mirror (same red, white and blue effect as Sal's eyebrows).

2    The footprints in the wash basin.

3    The heap of towels that was slowly soaking up the flood that . . .

4    . . . had been caused by somebody stuffing the shower curtain down the loo and pulling the chain.

The other thing that was a bit strange was there was no sign of little Tom. CLUMP CLUMP CLUMP. God, he was in the roof!

'Hold on, Tom,' I called, hurrying up the ladder and jamming my head and shoulder under the trap door. 'I'll have this open in a sec. I think it's a bit stuck.'

At that point, I heard something mumbling in the airing cupboard. I froze. It happened again. I was just going to climb down the ladder and check it out when I heard the muffled sound of a fist clumping on the trap door above my head. CLUMP CLUMP CLUMP.

'Wait up!' I yelled at the airing cupboard and smacked the trap door with the palms of both hands. That did it. It gave an inch and then opened all the way. 'You all right, Tom?' I asked. But it wasn't little Tom's pale face that peered down at me: it was Mum's.

'Where the heck have you been, Ben?' she yelled, practically knocking me into the bath in her hurry to get down the ladder. 'We've been trapped for ages! Didn't you hear us banging and calling?'

'Well, I . . .'

'My God! What's been going on in here!' She cut me off as she looked wildly about.

'Whew! I thought we'd never get out!' boomed Bunty's voice. Her huge pair of DMs appeared through the trap door – then a ginormous rear end in an Osh b'Gosh boiler suit. She gasped as she saw the mess but she was more worried about little Tom. 'What's happened to my baby!' she wailed feeling about in the weird-coloured water.

'It's OK,' I said. 'I don't think he's drowned.'

'Then where is he? Where is he?' she yelled.

'I couldn't swear to it but I think he's probably in the airing cupboard, actually.'

You'd have thought they would have been pleased by this brilliant bit of deduction but, no, it's all my fault again. Mum, who was nearest, snatched the door open and there was Tom wrapped from head to toe in toilet paper looking like a mini mummy from the Pharaoh's tomb.

'Tom got da bandads on,' piped up Nurse Sal from under the sink through her sucked thumb. 'Cos Niff bited him.'

Poor old Mum. She practically fainted at the thought of her friend's baby boy being

# Sniff and Sal's Invisible Friend

attacked by Sniff. 'Where did he bite him?' she said, frantically trying to unwrap the snivelling parcel.

'Bring him out on to the landing!' ordered Bunty. 'We can both get at him there.'

'I can't believe it! This carpet's almost as wet as the bathroom floor,' wailed Mum. 'Oo – I'll strangle Ben for this!'

'Why me . . . ?' I spluttered but she wasn't listening. She was helping Bunty strip away huge lengths of toilet roll. There was miles of it – and all the time, little Tom was just sort of humming and bubbling away. If you ask me, he thought it was ace being all bundled up, because he only let out a good window-rattling roar once the last few squares of loo paper had been stripped away. Mind you, I wouldn't be too chuffed to see Bunty hovering over me in a boiler suit waiting to smother me with love.

'Oh, that's it, sweetheart, don't bottle it up!' she cooed, jiggling him up and down while his little fists pounded on her head and he screamed his little lungs out. 'There, there, darling, Mummy's here.' Anyone except her could tell that that was what he was screaming about in the first place. It was ages before she could get any sense out of him. 'Did the doggy bite you, darling? Where did the doggy bite you? Show Mummy.' So we had to put up with WAH WAH and There There for another five minutes and he still wouldn't show anybody anything.

'I can't believe it,' Mum kept insisting between sobs. 'I can't believe it. Honestly, Bunty, Sniff's been such a good dog ... well, you know what I mean ... gentle. I trusted him absolutely and this is just awful. I just don't know what to say. Biting a *baby! It's just awful!* I'm so sorry ... I never imagined ...'

'He go RRRRAAAH!' said Sal helpfully, gnashing her teeth together. 'And he bited Zigzig and Zigzig go WHACK wid da lavvy brush on his head he did.'

'Bunty, I think the children must have upset him; it was too much for him ...'

'Something snapped. It happens sometimes, Jo, dear,' Bunty explained, rubbing Tom's heaving back while his feet pounded her chest. 'Animals all have this primitive streak, deep down.'

She was trying to cheer Mum up but Mum had gone all guilty. 'I shall have to call Robert. No, Ben – you phone Dad. Tell him it's an emergency. He's got to come home and deal with Sniff. Tell him what's happened – that he'll have to put Sniff away – in kennels or something. We can't have him here if he's going to start biting little babies.'

'What do you mean have him put away?' I yelled, dead upset. 'Have her put away!' I said, pointing at Sal. 'You heard her. She was the one who thumped him on the head with the lavvy brush.'

'Zigzig done dat!' screamed Sal.

So there was little Tom crying his head off, Mum crying, Bunty crying – even me, and I'm suppose to be hard and masculine and everything. Meanwhile, Sal had crawled out from under the washbasin and started looking at us all, one after the other, dead interested.

'So how come you and Bunty got stuck in the loft anyway?' I sniffed, trying to make Mum change the subject a bit.

'We were double-insulating,' Bunty answered for her. 'And one of the children must have climbed the ladder and pulled down the trap door-hor-hor.' Sob sob. Complete nervous breakdown.

'Go and phone Dad,' said Mum, wiping her eyes. 'The longer we put it off, the worse it's going to be.'

'I don't get it,' I said. 'Sniff's always getting knocked about and sat on and everything. But he's never bitten anybody before. Well, nobody small. Except the gas man, he's small, but he's a stranger. You've got to expect a dog to bite one or two strangers . . .' I knew I sounded desperate.

'Go on, Ben. He's done it now. He just can't be trusted any more.'

'Well, where? Go on, where?' I had one last go at making her see sense.

'Where what?'

'Where did he bite Tom?'

'He's got a point,' said Bunty. 'We haven't seen any marks yet. Show Mummy, Tom. Where did he bite you?' Little Tom's bottom lip came out about six inches and he pointed sadly at his chubby little leg.

Me and Mum held our breath as Bunty rolled up the leg of his track suit. And there it was – just below the knee, red tooth marks with little pinpricks of blood where the skin was broken.

Mum and Bunty looked shattered.

'Did da doddy do dat?' asked Sal sweetly, poking it with her index finger.

'Yaaah,' said little Tom, nodding his head.

'No he didn't!' I said, suddenly feeling like Inspector Morse and remembering my last fight with my darling little sister. I whipped up my sleeve and revealed an identical set of toothmarks. 'DA-DAAAAH!' I said.

Sal tried to claim it was Zigzig but it was obvious straight away that she was the phantom snapper. Mum and Bunty started cuddling each other and then passing Sal and Tom about and cuddling them like crazy. I told Mum to give Sal a good whack but she told me not to be ridiculous and shot downstairs to cuddle Sniff and tell him what a beautiful misunderstood gorgeous Mummy's special puppy wuppy he was.

So never mind about me being falsely accused of wrecking the bathroom. Never mind that Sal bit me to the bone and practically scratched my face off! I have to listen to Bunty and Mum giving me an anti-smacking lecture and telling me that the important thing is to reinforce the positive.

'Well can I have Streetfighter 3 then?' I said, thinking this was a good moment.

'You are so sneaky, Ben!' Mum says, and chucked a smelly old floorcloth at me.

She missed, but Sniff had had enough cuddling and stroking, so he grabbed it and charged over to smear me with it – all cold and stinky.

'Ahhh. Somebody loves you, Ben,' Mum said.

Sometimes I think I'm the only real adult in our whole family.

# Sniff Gets Stagestruck

SCENE: A school stage somewhere in England. 5.30 pm. Rehearsal for Oliver! A heroic band of young actors is being threatened because they make a titchy mistake in their singing of 'Food, Glorious Food' for the 798th time.

MR STAPLETON *(collapsing over piano keyboard)*: For crying out loud, Chorus! It is not 'Hot sausage and CUSTARD'!

CHORUS *(groan)*: Here we go.

MR STAPLETON: How many times have I got to tell you – it's 'Hot sausage and MUSTARD'? Now concentrate, Chorus, or I will kill you painfully one by one. And stop chewing. Shah – you're supposed to be starving in a workhouse, not hanging out in McDonalds! Shah's bare flat feet slapped across the stage as he went to bin his bubble gum. He looked such a prat in his pauper's costume that his mum had made too tight for his little fat arms and legs.

'Wait for it,' whispered Max. His held-back giggles were making our bench shake. Thurston had organized a joke with little paper cocktail umbrellas that depended on Mr Stapleton properly doing his nut. We'd had six weeks of boring rehearsal for Oliver!, six weeks of being forced to sing 'Food, Glorious Food' with a bunch of derrs who couldn't even wave their gruel bowls in time to the music. And just to make it worse as far as Thurston was concerned, Mr Stapleton had chosen Wells to star as Oliver instead of him. The only reason why Thurston had agreed to join Max and me and the other 'talentless peasants' in the chorus, was because he had this fantasy about stepping in and replacing Wells when the audience booed him off the stage on the first night. The other reason was to get his revenge on Mr Stapleton.

'Stand by for when he says "shambles",' whispered Thurston and we all had a little secret cocktail-umbrella-opening practice under our table.

You could see the balls of saliva that Mr Stapleton was famous for, gathering in the corners of his mouth. 'We've got exactly a week to get this shambles together!' he went, bang on cue.

Me, Max and Thurston whipped up our mini-brollies and held them over our heads, pretending to be sheltering from some huge showers of spit. The two Sixth Formers up

the ladder, fiddling with the safety chains on a spotlight above us, nearly fell off laughing and that made all the other kids turn round really fast to see what we were doing. We tried to look innocent but there's no way you can keep your face straight when Max's head is shaking like it's on a spring, and gunge is leaking out of his nose.

'I've had just about enough of you three!' snarled Mr Stapleton. 'Pests, the lot of you! So you can forget what I said about letting you do that pickpocket business in Fagin's Den. Kendle, Rose and Slifkin can do it.'

'Oh, Sir!' groaned Max. It was our only good bit – prancing about behind Fagin while he was singing 'You Gotta Picka Pocket or Two', showing Oliver how to nick silk hankies off posh people. It was a real laugh.

'They're useless, Sir,' squeaked Thurston. 'Well, Rose and Slifkin are, Sir.' He added the last bit because Kendle started threatening him with his wooden spoon.

'You don't have to tell me they're useless,'

snapped Mr Stapleton. 'I know they're useless. The whole lot of you are useless!' He
paced up and down, throwing his arms
about. 'None of you knows your lines – not
one of you! I can never get the whole cast
together. And those who do turn up behave
like tea-time at the monkey house! The blasted stage staff will only fix the lights while
I'm trying to rehearse! The Artful Dodger's
got a verucca and Watson is refusing to play
Nancy in a dress. So don't tell me Rose and
Slifkin are useless! At least I can trust them
not to smirk when smirking is uncalled for!'
snapped Mr Stapleton. 'Right, then . . . Slifkin
. . . where is Slifkin?'

No answer from Slifkin.

'Absent, Sir,' whispered somebody.

'Chicken pox, Sir,' murmured somebody
else.

'Spots all over, Sir.'

'Got it off Barber, Sir.'

'I don't believe it!' howled Mr Stapleton.
'Well, that just about takes the chocolate
digestive!' He flopped down on his stool and

slammed down the lid of the piano. We all jumped about a mile and listened nervously while the echoes of the BOINNNGGG gradually faded in the school hall. 'He's got no blasted business catching things off Barber! He's got solo bits in the first number, for a start. And he's the Knife Grinder in the street scene. And the drunk who falls over in "Oom Pa-Pa" . . . Oh, this is too much!' He looked as if he were going to cry.

'I'll do them, Sir!' yelled Max. 'I can do a brilliant drunk – look, Sir.' He chucked himself flat on his face so hard he made his nose bleed.

'No, me, Sir! I know those bits by heart, Sir, honestly, Sir,' crawled Thurston.

'Shut up!!' screamed Mr Stapleton. 'And stop bleeding all over the stage, that boy! Find a sink somewhere and bleed into it!' Max shuffled off towards the dressing rooms, holding his nose and trying to hum the Knife Grinder's tune at the same time, but Mr Stapleton wasn't even listening. He licked the ends of his fingers and started flip-

ping through the sheets of music like a mad-
man. Suddenly he saw something written
down and smacked himself right across the
forehead. 'Oh, my God! Slifkin's got the
screaming ab-dabs, and I was relying on him
to bring his bull terrier . . . so where in heav-
en's name are we going to find another one
to play Bullseye? If we haven't got a dog for
Bill Sikes, bang goes the whole of the last
scene! Bill's got to have the dog with him
when he murders Nancy – and the dog has
to lead the angry crowd to Bill's hideout just
before he gets shot. Right! That's it! The
show's off. Forget it. Push off, the lot of you –
it's all over!'

He laid his head in his arms on top of the
piano lid. And then he started banging his
head.

'Did you say "shot", Sir?' I said. 'Who gets
to shoot him?' Our bits only went up to
'Consider Yourself' in Act I when the Dodger
lets Oliver join Fagin's gang. It was all singing
and waving and galloping up and down with
the chorus – OK in its way – but not half as

good as shooting murderers, which sounded really ace.

'A hussar shoots him with a rifle, if you must know, Moore,' he mumbled.

Now I knew what that uniform was doing on a hanger at the back of the stage. It was wicked – bright blue with gold buttons and this tall hat like the bloke on the Quality Street packet! I could just see myself, with all the audience going – 'Look at that kid in the dead smart costume! Check out that wicked gun!' and sticking their fingers in their ears as I take aim at Bill Sikes . . . and BLAM! – all the little kids starting to cry and everything. Wow, I just had to have that part.

'Was Slifkin going to be the hussar, as well as all those other bits, Sir?' I asked.

'As a matter of fact he was, though why you're wasting everybody's time with these questions, I just don't . . .'

'I've got a dog, Sir,' I said. 'He's a really good actor.'

Mr Stapleton sat up straight and looked at me dead interested. Max and Thurston looked well gutted. Then Mr Stapleton opened the piano lid, stretched out his arms into the conducting position and said hopelessly: 'Once more, Chorus, from the top . . . "Food, Glorious Food" . . .'

'Not exactly a bull terrier, is it?' said Mr Stapleton – the following day, half an hour before morning registration. He was calmer now, but he still didn't look what you might call confident. I'd brought Sniff round to the practice room behind the Music School to introduce him.

'He can act quite fierce, though, Sir,' I said.

Sniff was trying to lick off a gob of chewing gum that some kid must have parked under the piano while he was practising. I dragged him away and pointed him at Mr Stapleton. He dribbled a bit.

'Terrifying,' said Mr Stapleton. 'And you say you can train him for the part in a week?'

'Definitely, Sir,' I said. 'He's incredibly intelligent.'

'Will he allow Singh to handle him?' he

wondered. Singh was this Monitor who was playing Bill Sikes, a dead hard kid who had to shave and everything. He had this really stubbly chin, looked a bit like Bluto off Popeye. I liked Singh, even though he'd given me a couple of Monitors' detentions for cheek, and he was a wicked actor. I'd seen him in a House play, doing one of the Romans who stab Julius Caesar – not Brutus – one of those other more sneaky ones who get him in the back.

'Sniff gets on with everybody, Sir, 'specially if he's on a lead. And if I was somewhere nearby, Sir, keeping an eye on him, Sir, when Bill Sikes is on stage – like, maybe like one of Bill Sikes's gang or something . . .'

'Sikes is rather a loner, Moore.'

'Ah. Well how about one of the people of London – just sort of hanging about nearby, Sir. Like a hussar, sort of thing.'

'As I explained yesterday, the hussar will be required to fire a blank from a rifle. It's potentially rather dangerous, you know, Moore. Are you sure you can handle the responsibility? Will you be able to keep an eye on the dog and concentrate on the rifle at the same time?'

'Honestly, Sir, you don't need to worry about it, Sir,' I said. 'You'll be all right with me and Sniff.'

Mum and Dad said that it would probably be best just to get Sniff used to all the people for the first visit.

So I took him along on the Tuesday, when they were doing some of the Bill Sikes scenes, and he was quite happy just padding up and down the hall, nosing out the odd bit of school dinner that had rolled out of sight of the cleaners, and bouncing off to meet anyone who whistled or slipped him a Hula Hoop. Singh gave him half a Mars Bar, so Sniff thought he was a real hero and followed him to heel – no lead or anything – right through the dressing rooms behind the stage, out on to the left side of the stage, up the steps across the scaffolding that was going to be London Bridge, down the steps on the other side and through the right exit. Brill! I was really proud of him.

'Fine. Get the dog on a rope or something and we'll try the murder, then,' said Mr Stapleton. 'Moore, you'll be strolling across the bridge first in your hussar uniform – just to set the scene.'

'Will I have my gun, Sir?' I said. 'Because how about I just take a potshot at a pigeon or a seagull or something? That way, everybody will get the idea he's ...'

'Absolutely not, Moore,' Mr Stapleton interrupted. 'No gun, no bangs till right at the end. You're supposed to be just out for a midnight stroll on London Bridge, for Pete's sake, not charging about in Dodge City. Let's not confuse the issue.'

'How about if I smoke a pipe, Sir, and look dead casual?'

'No, you are blinking well not smoking a pipe, Moore. You just stroll across and you can give Nancy and Oliver a nice little salute as you pass. I don't want you making a meal of it. Got that?'

I thought the pipe idea was brill, but I just said 'Yes, Sir,' because he was starting to get wiggy again.

'So, Oliver,' went on Mr Stapleton, pointing so that Wells could see what he was talking about, 'you come down the steps ahead of Nancy. It's midnight, pitch dark, so you feel your way along by that pillar – feel feel feel – don't dash at it. Bill Sikes is hiding in the gap there – with the dog. Right? Bill jumps out and grabs Oliver. You have a struggle. Nancy screams, runs back up the steps. Bill, you knock Oliver down, chase after Nancy, catch her at the top of the steps and – whack whack whack – bludgeon the life out of her . . .'

'What with, Sir?' grinned Singh.

'With a bludgeon, you fool. We'll get you one. Just get on with it and murder her – because if you don't, I will.'

'That's not fair, Sir,' whined Watson. 'I said I'd wear a dress on the night.'

'Yes, Watson, so you did. You also said you could act. You're supposed to be a desirable female, not centre half for Millwall! So start focusing, laddy!'

Then Mr Stapleton got the lighting staff to fade the lights and Singh started practising creeping about under the scaffolding and dodging behind a pillar with Sniff on a rope – well, his House tie, actually. I marched over the bridge, gave this wicked salute to Watson and Wells – who hardly even looked at me. I could see why Mr Stapleton was worried about the show, because they were rubbish – completely unbelievable. Anyway, they got their moves more or less right up to the point where Bill Sikes grabs Oliver. Then Sniff went a bit berserk like he always does if he sees people having pretend fights. Then Wells said Sniff had gone for him.

'They've over-excited him, Sir,' I called to Mr Stapleton. 'Tell them to keep the struggle down a bit. Don't take any notice of Wells, Sir. It won't have been more than a nip.'

From what I could see with the lights down low, Mr Stapleton was looking rather pleased. 'Just get on with bludgeoning Nancy,

Singh,' he called out. 'I've got a million other things to worry about tonight.'

'What if the dog goes for me, like he did for Wells?' wailed Watson.

'He won't hurt you, you big girlie!' shouted Mr Stapleton. 'Get on with it, laddy! Realism! Realism!'

'Stage Manager wants to know will this do for a bludgeon, Sir?' asked Singh. 'It's a stuffed sock.'

'Stuffed with what?' wailed Watson.

'Do shut up and get yourself in position to get murdered, Watson!' yelled Mr Stapleton. 'And stop being a wet week at Skegness!'

'I'll distract Sniff, Sir, from the wings, Sir,' I called. 'Got any of that Mars Bar left, Singhie? I'll wave it from over here behind the curtain while you whack Watson.'

That worked OK. Singh made dead meat of Watson with the stuffed sock and Sniff didn't even give them a glance. He was all of a tremble, looking the other way, listening to me crinkling the Mars Bar wrapper. Next thing he knew, Singh was tugging at the tie and dragging him off the other side of the stage.

'How did that look, Sir,' asked Singh, coming back on stage and squinting under his hand out towards Mr Stapleton.

'On a scale of one to ten, I give that nought-point-five for performance,' sighed Mr Stapleton. 'And to think the Governors are coming on the opening night! My reputation as a producer is about to be slooshed down the plughole, thanks to you lot!'

'That really hurt, Singh!' Watson complained. 'They've got something really hard in that sock, Sir, like conkers, Sir.'

'Lighting Manager!' yelled Mr Stapleton, ignoring him.

'Sir?' came a muffled shout from the lighting room.

'Bring the lighting right down through that scene. Our only hope here is to leave most of what's going on to the audience's imagination.'

'Was Sniff OK, Sir?' I said, coming down to sit on the edge of the stage.

'No comment,' sighed Mr Stapleton.

The Dress Rehearsal was rubbish – or the parts I saw were, anyway, except for Sniff and me. Sniff was dead obedient. He followed Bill Sikes about like Mary's little lamb, he didn't bite anybody, and he just went quietly along with the crowd when they were chasing Bill. And when I pointed the rifle at Bill and pulled the trigger and there was this wicked bang – Sniff didn't jump about or anything. He just sat quiet, like he was acting upset at the death of his naughty old master. Maybe the fact that he'd raided the dustbin at home and eaten a whole tub of taramasalata that had been hidden at the back of the fridge for about three years had something to do with him being so sort of droopy and calm. I did notice him chucking up into Fagin's slippers in the dressing room afterwards. The kid who was playing Fagin was getting his false nose glued on at the time, so I cleaned most of the sick out with a Hula Hoop packet and Fagin didn't suspect a thing.

We finished at about 11 o'clock at night

and Mr Stapleton looked well wiped out. He said that, apart from the fact that he couldn't hear any of the words, that nobody remembered any of their moves, that nobody could act for toffee, that the band couldn't keep together, and that the lighting and scenery were rubbish – it was a great show.

Typical. He didn't say a thing about how brilliant the shooting bit was.

'Get away from those curtains, you boys! The audience can see you!' hissed Mr Stapleton. 'Go and wait in the dressing room with the rest! And, Moore, do something about that wretched dog. He's upsetting the make-up ladies.'

'Is that the Chairman of the Governors with the red nose, Sir?' asked Thurston, still squinting through the gap in the curtains.

'He's not here already, is he?' groaned Mr Stapleton, pushing Thurston aside to look. 'Heaven help us!'

'Take a look at Mr Reed, Sir,' said Max. 'Is that his girlfriend sitting next to him with the miniskirt and the nose-rings, Sir?'

'Where?' said Mr Stapleton. 'Oh, I say . . .'
Then he remembered and started flapping
again. 'Five minutes. Get off the stage and
stand by! And tell that lot back there to keep
quiet! I've got to get out front to conduct the
Overture and . . . Good Grief, Wilder! Who on
earth did your make up?'

'I did, Sir,' smirked Thurston. 'Rather radical,
wouldn't you say, Sir? I was after a haunted
and under-nourished look. I made all the boils
out of nose-putty, Sir.'

'You're supposed to be a nineteenth cen-
tury urchin in a workhouse, not a victim of
bubonic plague, laddy! Just get Miss Press to
fix it, quick! And Oliver . . . !' (Wells had just
come on stage for a sneaky peek at the audience.) '. . . you get off as well, and leave your
something-something wristwatch in the
changing room!' Mr Stapleton grabbed it off
him, shoved us into the wings and dashed off
to start the music.

'Dead unprofessional,' said Thurston.
'Getting in a panic like that. And as for you,

Wells, you slab of fossiliferous oolite, Stapleton must have been off his head to pick you as the star.' Wells just grinned and went to talk to Lomax.

'And I'd have made a better Artful Dodger than Lomax an' all,' moaned Max. 'He ain't even got the accent right.'

'Let's face it, the show is doomed,' said Thurston. 'I wouldn't fancy being in Mr Stapleton's shoes, I'll tell you that, not with the Governors out there taking notes.'

'D'you reckon they'll sack him?' asked Max.

'Practically a certainty,' said Thurston. 'National Curriculum and all that.'

'Wo!' said Max who's impressed by anything over two syllables.

'Here, Ben,' said Thurston, changing the subject quickly. 'What say we go outside and see if your rifle's working?'

'We can't,' I said. 'Stapleton's told the Stage Manager to hang on to it till just before the bit where I fire it.'

'Bummer!' said Thurston and Max together.

Suddenly the lights went dim and the orchestra started playing the Overture so slowly it sounded like something needed oiling. We were off! Quick, no time to see Miss Press about Thurston's boils. What about Sniff? Who was keeping an eye on him? Too late to worry about that. Where the heck was the rest of the Chorus? It was 'Food, Glorious Food' time. The first half couldn't have been worse. The lighting was so dim, everybody kept bashing into everybody else. Mr Bumble forgot his lines. Fagin's nose fell off in the middle of 'You've got to pick a pocket or two' and he told me in the interval that he was going to push my face in for letting my dog puke in his slippers.

'Nightmare!' wailed Mr Stapleton, bursting into the changing room. 'It's a shambles! Put some life into it, some of you, before the entire audience falls asleep!'

Singh had run out of cheese and onion crisps by the interval and Sniff was pretty obviously losing interest in him. He'd chewed his lead – which was a shame because it was a nice dickensy-looking thing I'd made out of the cord from Dad's pyjamas. And Miss Press was on the warpath because he'd put his paws in the face powder and had left paw-prints all over most of the costumes.

I'd just done my bridge crossing in my hussar outfit, and I was watching Sniff performing, while trying to stop the stage hands from grabbing my rifle. I could tell by the sort of growly-whiny noises he was making, that Sniff's concentration was going. It was probably sicking up that bad taramasalata all the night before that was making him extra hungry.

You could hear the audience beginning to murmur with fright when Bill Sikes lifted his stuffed sock to whack Nancy – and then Sniff went completely bonkers! He bit Nancy, then took a flying leap at Oliver. Oliver (Wells) panicked, started screaming his head off and legged it into the wings. Sniff struggled so hard to get after him that his chewed lead snapped. Bill Sikes made the mistake of raising his stuffed sock in the air to try to calm him down and Sniff went for it, knocking Bill against the bridge in the process. Bits of scenery that were tacked to the scaffolding began to rain down on him and Bill and Nancy. Sniff dived out from under like a rescue worker after an earthquake, and started tearing at the sheets of painted hardboard with his teeth and claws. Bill Sikes emerged from the debris, and staggered to his feet. He decided to run for his life, but he could see his way off to the wings was blocked by Sniff, so there was only one thing for it – to run forwards.

I could guess where Singhy was heading. He jumped off the front of the stage and ran for it up the centre aisle. Everybody in the audience jumped up and yelled 'Get him, boy! Kill!' and, as bad old Bill Sikes ran towards the Exit sign with Sniff after him, suddenly, out of the darkness and into the spotlight on the stage appeared . . . Yessss! a hussar with a rifle.

'Stoppeth in the name of the Law!' I

ordered, making up my lines on the spot. Singh kept going. 'Then eateth lead, thou Bludgeoner!' I yelled and let him have it. BLAM! I bet a load of educated people in the audience thought that was straight out of Charles Dickens.

As soon as Sniff realized it was me, he did a skid-turn and came rushing back down the aisle with his tongue streaming out, partly to give me a good licking and partly because, even from thirty metres away, he could spot the Snickers bar that I was cunningly waving at him. Singhy had the good sense to let out a mega death-scream and collapse against the exit doors, and the Stage Manager had the good sense to close the curtains fast. WILD APPLAUSE!

'Not quite the ending I had in mind, but effective nonetheless,' was Mr Stapleton's verdict. The Chairman of the Governors had already been backstage with the Head to congratulate us all on a most excellent and original interpretation of the play.

'Same again tomorrow night?' smiled Mr

Stapleton to the cast.

Singh grinned and said 'Why not?' but, for some strange reason, Watson and Wells weren't all that keen!

'Well, in that case, we shall just have to call on some understudies,' said Mr Stapleton. 'Where's that boy with the boils and his freckly friend? You two all right for Oliver and Nancy tomorrow?'

'No thanks, Sir. Kind of you to recognize our talent, but we're needed in the Chorus,' said Thurston hastily. 'Eh, Max?'

'Food, Glorious Food!' sang Max, nearly in tune. Anything to get out of putting on a dress and appearing on a stage with Sniff.

# Sniff Makes You Wonder

Sometimes Sniff does stuff that makes you wonder if he just pretends he's only got about two brain cells. Like on the first day of Half Term. Mind you, I started off being sure he was just plain stupid.

'You are going,' insisted Dad, clattering his dirty plate into the bottom of the dishwasher. 'You can be there before one o'clock. It's still only half past twelve.'

'But why me? I had nothing to do with it!' I said.

'Just look at the state of that dog,' said Dad.

Mum yelled, 'Sal! Come and eat your lunch now!'

'Stupid animal!' I said.

Sniff was lying under the kitchen table. A fair amount of him was a sort of orangey-red, and he had one green ear and one yellow one. Apart from that and two or three bald patches on his back, I s'pose you could say he looked just his normal scruffy self.

'You can't expect Sal to take him – and you helped her to deface the dog,' said Mum, scraping baked beans next to the fish fingers in Sal's Peter Rabbit bowl.

'All I did was leave the dishwasher door open, Mum! I don't see how you can call that helping her,' I said. 'Anyway, you know what Sniff's like with Sal. He lets her beat him up. He's so stupid . . .'

'I've told you a dozen times that if you leave the door down,' Mum droned on, 'a certain little person can pull out the drying racks, climb up into the sink, crawl across the draining board, and then right along the work surfaces. Then that certain little person can reach all kinds of dangerous things . . . the m-a-t-c-h-e-s, for example. Not to mention bottles of cake colouring and the kitchen s-c-i-s-s-o-r-s!'

'I diddung cline up dare,' said Sal, shaking her head, all innocent.

'Oh, I get it,' I said. 'It was Zigzig. Your Invisible Friend climbed up and got the scissors and the cake colouring and then climbed down and tried them out on Sniff.' Sal took her thumb out just long enough to say, 'You shaddup bogy boy' and stuck it back again. 'Ben!' said Dad, getting my neck in a death-grip. 'Very bad language for the under-threes!'

'What?' I said. 'She learnt that at Play School, not off me!'

Sal squatted down behind Sniff who was concentrating on a pea that had got wedged under the dishwasher. He was doing such a lot of huffing that, if you didn't know him, you'd have thought he was trying to suck it up his nose. Sal didn't like him ignoring her. She grabbed him by the tail and hoiked him across the tiles. Mum squealed at her to be gentle with doggies because they might bite.

Not Sniff. He turned round and gave her a great slobbery kiss across the chops. She took a swing at him with her free fist, missed, banged her head on the table leg, tripped over, fell flat on her back and started to scream.

'You want to watch it, Sal,' I said. 'If the postman comes by and sees that mouth, he'll put a parcel in there!'

'Right, Ben, time to suffer,' said Dad.

'Why me?' I said. 'All I did was go and watch Neighbours and forget to close the door of the flipping dishwasher!'

'Exactly my point,' said Dad. 'You will pay for this crime in a suitably painful and educational manner. One: you are going to take the dog to the poodle parlour. Two: my enquiries have led me to believe that they will charge twenty-five quid for restoring the dog's dignity; that will be coming out of the Benjamin Moore Nintendo Fund . . .'

'Oh that's just great . . .' I said.

I decided to disguise myself as a French kid, because if anybody thought I had decorated the dog, I didn't want them to know it was me . . . if you get what I mean. And besides, I didn't want people to think that I was the type of kid who would normally be seen in a poodle parlour – apart from if I crash-landed into it after bailing out of a burning Tornado F3 or something.

It took me ages to find a beret and a bow tie because I was blowed if I was going to ask Mum and Dad to help, what with them being so unfair and everything. So I had a good old rummage in their bedroom and finally dug out what I needed, including Mum's sunglasses. Then I remembered Sherlock Holmes telling Doctor Watson that the perfect disguise depends on attention to detail, so I slapped on a handful of Dad's 'Monsieur Sexy' after-shave. Finally, I nipped downstairs and ate a teaspoonful of garlic mayonnaise. Nice one!

Sniff was dead embarrassed about being seen in public all orange and green and bald in patches, which I thought served him right for being so stupid and getting me into this mess. Lucky for him there weren't that many people about just after lunch on Monday afternoon, even at Half Term. I had to drag him most of the way to the High Street, and once he got a whiff of Muckypups, he went rigid and I had to pick him up and struggle with him in my arms to the door.

There was a customer sitting in the shop under a sign that said Welcome Paws and Claws. You could tell she was going to cause trouble, just by the way she looked at us. She had one of those snarly little terriers on her knee, the kind Sniff hates. She was wearing a plastic apron with a picture of a poodle on the chest, and underneath it said 'I heart muckypups'. No way were they going to get me to wear one of those, even if I was brilliantly disguised as a foreigner.

I pushed the door open with my shoulder about half an inch, and straight away, the titchy dog went bananas . . . squirming and snarling, rolling his mean little eyes and showing his nasty pointy teeth. On his own turf, Sniff would have had him for breakfast, but he didn't fancy the set-up here one little bit. He straightened his front legs against my chest and pushed. I toppled over backwards and he legged it as fast as he could, dragging me sideways over the paving stones as I hung on to his lead.

I was still stretched out on the pavement in front of Muckypups, trying to keep my arms in their sockets, when the shop-owner, a ginormous, droopy red-faced bloke with a face like a boiled St Bernard, came fizzing out. 'Oy!' he yelled. You don't go round with a dog like Sniff without getting a few Oys

now and again, but you don't expect them from people you're just going to pay twenty-five quid. 'Shove off,' he said, threatening us with a hairbrush.

'Mais, Monsieur . . .' I stuttered.

'What are they – punks?' yelled the lady with the yappy terrier as Sniff and I got more and more tangled up in his lead. I sensed that another kid had turned up and was standing behind us, but I was too busy rolling about on the pavement to see who it was.

'Couple of them tearaways!' said the owner. 'Them Grunges. Troublemakers, any-

way! And if you don't put your tongue in, son, I shall get my shears out and snip the end orf!' Put whose tongue away? I had no idea what he was going on about.

'A short sharp shock – that'd soon sort them lot out!' yelled the old lady. She had to yell to make herself heard above the Yip! Yip! Yip! of her horrible dog. 'And just look what this one's done to his poor animal! A disgrace that is, giving a dumb animal a punk hairdo like that! He wants the RSPVC after him. They'd give what for!'

'Excusez-moi, Monsieur,' I puffed. Sniff was sort of hypnotized by the hairbrush and stood still, staring at it, so I carried on ... 'Parlez-vous français? Non? Un peu? Non? Bon.'

'What are you on about?' said the man.

'Mon chien ici avez ad un accidonc,' I said. 'Voulez-vous fixie? Avez-vous un petit shampoo? Et un petit snippy-snip all round est un bon idea – oui?'

'I'll give you snippy-snip!' roared the bloke. 'Hop it. You're upsetting my regulars! And take your wouf-wouf and your rude friend with you before I sort out the lot of you!'

Rude friend? I looked behind me and saw this dazed-looking, ginger-haired kid with his tongue sticking out. It was Max!

'Put your tongue in, Max,' I said. 'He's not kidding.'

'Can't elk it,' said Max. 'Nettol.'

'Dettol?' I said, getting hold of his arm and steering him down the street out of harm's way. 'On your tongue?' He nodded like mad. 'Your mum?' He nodded again.

Poor old Max. She's a nightmare, his mum. That's one of her punishments, dipping his tongue in Dettol.

'Let's get out of here,' I said, and we legged it as far as the bridge by the fish shop, and by then Max had managed to get his tongue back in. 'Hey, Max, you OK?' I puffed.

'Yeah,' he breathed. 'You don't half look a prat.' He was back to normal, then. I explained about Sal and the scissors and the cake colouring and my disguise and every-thing. He told me he recognized me straight away and I said, 'What, even with the after shave and garlic breath?' and he admitted that, OK, those were nice little touches.

'So why the Dettol treatment?' I said, sticking the beret and the shades in my pockets. Instead of answering, he pointed to his nose. 'What?' I said, trying to see. All I could make out was a load of freckles. He leaned really close and pointed at his right nostril. Sniff got interested and jumped up and licked it. 'Pack it in!' said Max to Sniff, and then to me, 'That's a hole.'

''Course it is,' I said. 'It's called a nostril.'

'Very funny,' said Max. 'I'm talking about the hole for a nose-ring – there, look!'

'What'd you want to do that for?' I asked. 'You know your nose is always running.'

'I done it to spite my mum, 'coz she's always making me get my hair cut,' he sulked.

'It's only a dent,' I said, giving it a close look. 'I don't think it goes right through. What did you do it with?'

'Cor, your breath!' Max said. Then he said,

'I done it with a drawing pin, nearly killed meself. But my mum said it served me right and got hold of me and put Dettol on it in case it went bad and then she Dettolled me tongue. I hate her. And no way am I getting my hair cut.'

'God, you're really stubborn, Max,' I said. 'You know she'll kill you. How can you be so stupid?'

'Who you callin stupid?' snarled Max, getting really egged up.

By now, we'd passed the fish shop, the chemist, the fireplace shop and we were up as far as Jimmy's Unisex Hair Salon. Jimmy was sitting outside, reading The Sun.

'Hey, boyss, boyss! Nobody's stupid, OK?' He folded up his newspaper, smiled and tapped us both on the head with it. He's a great bloke, looks a bit like that guy in Bay Watch, only Greek, if you know what I mean. I mean, if you got knocked off your surf board by a giant wave, you wouldn't feel too bad about getting rescued by somebody like Jimmy. 'Wassup?' he said to Max who just jerked an angry thumb at his hair. 'Mum says must have haircut and joo don't want? Yes, I know this problem.' 'I still ain't havin' one,' mumbled Max.

'Got to admit, iss a bit stringly round joo collar,' smiled Jimmy. 'I give you nice trim, yess? No waiting – business not good today! Ah, allo poochy!' Sniff came out from behind my legs. He got the old tail going and started bouncing off Jimmy, whimpering and wiggling with pleasure. A lot of other people would have made cleverdick remarks about the state of him, but Jimmy just said, 'Ah, joo can smell my dogss! Yess! Clever boy!'

'I wouldn't call him clever,' I said.

'Oh yes. Iss very intelligent in the eyes. Some sheepssdog in him maybe?'

'What dogs have you got, then?' I said, noticing the expert way he had of making Sniff squirm with a tickle here, a rub there.

'Gun dogss,' said Jimmy. 'Retrieverss. Also very bright, very clever. I tell you samthin. When me an my friendss go shootin in Sunday morninss – if I late, one of my dogss go in back room and bring me box of cartridges. Ee say, "Cam on, Jimmy – you forget we goin out?" And if I lookin to light the kettle, he fetch the matches! No kiddin!'

'Is that right?' said Max.

'God'ss honour,' said Jimmy. He ran his hand along Sniff's back. 'He's havin accident, I see . . .'

'It was my little sister . . .' I said and Jimmy nodded. He understood. He put his hand under Sniff's chin and tilted up his head.

'See the shape of his skull? Means big brainss. Iss very obedient, yess? He does some tricks?'

I couldn't think of anything brainy Sniff had ever done, or any tricks, just at that moment. I opened my mouth but nothing came out.

'OK, I tell joo samthin, boyss. I very depress. No customer, nathin doin. So come inside and I give nice 50p shampoos and trim, eh-? Would be my pleasure. I got special jollopss – no sting the eyesss.'

'Cor!' said Max, thinking it would be

worth having a haircut if there was some change in it. He got ready to go in.

'Er . . . actu-alee,' said Jimmy. 'I was talkin about special jollopss for dogss, for him there.' He pointed to Sniff but then he must have seen the disappointment in Max's face, because he added. 'OK, dogss first, joo next!'

'I don't think . . .' I was going to say I didn't think Sniff was too keen on any kind of jollop (whatever that is), unless it's the sort you can roll in – but, amazingly, Sniff followed Jimmy into the shop as if he was following a trail of Doggy Chocs.

'Hup!' said Jimmy, and Sniff jumped into the chair nearest the window. 'Hup!' he said again, and Sniff hopped into the sink. 'Joo got to remember with dogss,' said Jimmy, pouring brown jollop out of a jar into the palm of his hand and turning on the taps for the spray, 'that sometimes dogs is very, very shy.' I couldn't believe Sniff was just sitting there, letting himself be shampooed!

'So, very important they trust you. My dogsss just same as yours. So I mix little bit

shampoo, little bit horsypoo, little bit cow-
poo – and no problemss! They love it!'

It was ace! There should have been cam-
eras recording it! Jimmy lathered Sniff, and
Sniff enjoyed himself having a good slurp at
the tasty lather. Next, Jimmy rinsed him off
and combed out the lumps of Blutak that Sal
had used to try and stick some of his fur back
on with. Then with a snip here and a snip
there, he started to level things off a bit. He
managed to lose most of the bald patches by
re-directing the rest of the fur. Sniff was well
chuffed to see something like his mad old
hairy self in the mirror and let rip with a

RRRAALPH! RRRAALPH! But there was nobody around to appreciate what a great barber Jimmy was – apart from him, me and Max. 'Wicked, Jimmy!' I said, really gob-smacked. Sniff had never kept still for that long in his life. 'Here. My Dad gave me £25 to get him done at Muckypups. You have it.'

'Thank you, no. 50p only,' said Jimmy, holding up his hand like a traffic policeman. 'Bargainss iss bargainss, OK? Next please!' Sniff jumped down, shook himself into shape and had a good nose round the shop while Max stepped into the chair. Jimmy had started to tell us about Cyprus, the sunshine, the brilliant vegetables they grew where he lived. 'If joo are friend of the cucumber, joo come to my village,' he said. 'Iss delicioosss – and lotss friendly people all the time ...'

The phone rang and he answered it in Greek. Soon he was getting well egged up, waving his free arm about and talking nine-teen to the dozen. He took a packet of fags out of his shirt pocket and started patting his other pockets, looking for matches. There was a box on the counter by the till – red ones, in a box with a map of Cyprus on one side. I was just going to chuck it to Jimmy when I suddenly had this vision in my mind of Sniff doing something dead obedient and intelligent. I closed the box and shook it under Sniff's nose. 'Take these to Jimmy,' I said. 'Show him what a clever boy you are. Off you go, boy. Fetch!'

I opened his jaws, put the box between his teeth and closed them again. Sniff sat down, rolled his eyes and looked puzzled. 'Show Uncle Jimmy your trick,' I said. 'Go on – fetch.'

Jimmy saw what I was up to, winked, without stopping his conversation and started flipping his fingers at Sniff. Straight away, Sniff dropped the box between his front paws and attacked it. He shook it, tossed it up in the air, caught it – and chewed the life out of it. Or he would have done, if the box hadn't burst into flames.

Sniff went YIKE! and charged off into the far corner of the shop to hide behind the laundry basket while Max and I stamped on the flames. I expected Jimmy to go mad – but he laughed, shouted something very excited into the phone and put it down.

He marched straight over to the corner and started making a fuss of Sniff. He found his happy spot, just behind his ears, and in about ten seconds flat. Sniff was out from behind the laundry basket, lying on his back offering his tum for a tickle. 'Smart boy!' smiled Jimmy. 'In just a couple minutes we see how smart! And while we wait – I finish trim for Ginger, OK?'

'OK,' said Max. 'But not too much off the back.'

'We all got some problemss today, eh?' smiled Jimmy, getting busy with the scissors. 'I tell you what, boyss,' he grinned. 'I trying all week to give up the cigarettes. I think your dog know that. Iss damn clever thing he done to stop me!'

The phone rang. Jimmy spoke Greek for a second, then he jumped into the air and shouted Yess!

'Was Chris Christou from White Tower Restaurant,' he smiled, replacing the receiver. 'He talkin to me before about bettin on the horses. I told him I got no customers, I got no money. He say is OK – he put on ten pounds for me if I say the horse. I say I don't know the horse to win. And then this very intelligent dog tell me. He tell me "Smoke Signal"! So I say to Chris, "Smoke Signal is runnin in 12.40? OK put ten pounds on Smoke Signal for me." Now Chris is call back to say Smoke Signal win by three lengths at 10 to 1!'

'Wicked!' said me and Max, thinking 'A hundred quid! Wow!'

'What are you going to do with your change?' I asked Max as we were going past the baker's on our way home.

'I think I'll buy me mum some of them gooey cakes there,' said Max. 'And then eat the lot meself. How about you?'

'Nintendo fund,' I said. Sniff had spotted a pile of cream doughnuts. He started whining and scratching at the window.

'You don't think Jimmy's right, Max?' I said.

'What about Sniff being intelligent?' said Max. 'Naah ... I mean that was all luck, what happened in Jimmy's, wasn't it?'

'S'pose so,' I said.

'I mean, look at him, will ya?' said Max. Long strings of drool were dangling from Sniff's chops and his eyes were crossed. He stepped back a couple of paces to get the doughnuts in focus, then jumped at them and bonged his nose on the window so hard that it rattled.

A lady in a pink striped overall came running out of the shop. Oh, no! I thought. Here we go again! I braced myself for her to start having a real go at us.

'Ah, poor thing!' she said. She reached into her pocket and pulled out a handful of something. Like a flash, Sniff was up and begging. 'Who's a clever boy, then?' she crooned. Even Max was impressed by the fact that Sniff was soon crunching away at about half a pound of sugared almonds.

'How does he do it?' he said in my ear.

'Makes you wonder, doesn't it?' I said.

# Sniff and the Laptop

There was only one good thing about everybody in our class having to write their autobiography over the weekend – Max was going to get a well good sorting out on Monday. He'd been so busy drawing a picture on my English folder of me having my intestines torn out by a raptor, he'd missed what Cleggy said we were supposed to do. So at the end of the lesson, when he was asking Thurston what the homework was, I said to him, 'Max, you are so sad. Don't you even know what an autobiography is?' That shut him up. It was going to be a good laugh on Monday morning when he turned up with a nice little story about the life of a Ford Escort.

In the meantime, it was Sunday morning, the weather was great for mucking about with the lads down the woods or something. And I was having a bad time with The Life of Benjamin Moore. Complete bummer. I just couldn't get started at all. The trouble with my parents is that when you ask a simple question like 'What happened in my life?', it's like turning on a tap, but it's all the wrong stuff. It's all dead boring – like how much I weighed at birth and how my face looked all squashed and how important it was that I was born at home, where I could feel secure and rooted. It turns out Mum had this fight with Doctor Nelki when she found out she was pregnant and absolutely refused to let me be born in a proper hygienic hospital. God, how could I put that in an essay? Cleggy would probably make me read it out in front of the whole class! It could even make the school newsletter. DOCTOR WARNED MOORE FAMILY OF KILLER-DUST IN HOME.

Then Mum and Dad started going on

about how amazingly beautiful my placenta was and how Dad cried and how Bunty lit a joss stick to make sure my karma was OK or something. 'Bunty?' I said. I was dead shocked. They'd never mentioned this before. I could just imagine her there, wearing her headband and her ding-dongy flares and her cardigan with all the little bits of mirror on it, and going all soppy. 'How could you let her be there in your bedroom? Do you mean to say she was the first thing I saw in the whole world?' I said. So embarrassing.

'Bunty has always been a very loyal friend,' Mum said. 'She'd spent weeks composing a very special song to celebrate your arrival and she performed it for us before the midwife cut the cord.'

'I don't believe it! What do you mean "performed"? You don't mean – with a guitar and everything!'

'And a harmonica,' said Dad. 'It had a touch of Bob Dylan about it.'

'If any of this gets out, I swear I'll kill myself,' I said.

Mum told me that if I was going to be melodramatic I could flipping well invent a life of my own and stormed off with Dad to check out the nettles at the top end of the garden.

I got myself a sheet of paper and started drawing little Marios in the margin just to start me off. Then I wrote My Hobbies and My Phobias and My Family and My Worst Accident but that was just depressing because I'd done all them about a billion times for different teachers. So I went over the letters, to make them look more interesting, and put curly bits on the capitals, and then more and more until you could hardly see they were letters at all. Then I put my biro up my nose and that reminded me of when I had to go to Doctor Nelki when I was seven to have him remove a smelly rubber from my ear. It was in the shape of one of those little blackcurrant guys they have on the Ribena adverts. I had a whole sweet jar full of different little cute things like that. Doctor Nelki told Mum they could be lethal if I swallowed one, so what did she do? She crept into my room in the middle of the night and took them away. I went mad for weeks, convinced that the little Ribena guys had probably marched off to Ribena Land to punish me for insulting one of their men by sticking him in my ear. Two years later, Mum confessed she'd done it to save me from an early grave. I was really gutted. I told her she'd probably twisted something really important in my personality . .

So I was doodling and thinking all these wandering thoughts when it clicked . . . how to make my job much easier. I went charging up the garden and found Mum and Dad pulling bindweed out from among the nettles to give the nettles a chance. I thought I'd better soften them up by showing an interest in the garden so I said, 'How can you say this is a conservation area if you start interfering with Nature?'

'We're compromising,' Dad said. 'Mum gets her butterflies and I keep the blasted bindweed out of my beanrows.'

'Not just butterflies,' Mum said. 'Bunty and I thought we'd investigate their properties as fibre for material. Apparently they made trousers for the German Army out of nettles during the War.'

'Ah, that explains the goose-step,' I said. 'By the way, I'm just borrowing your laptop to write my autobiography?'

That wiped the smile off Dad's face. 'No you're blinking well not!' he said. 'Strictly speaking, that's college property, and it cost three and a half thousand.'

'Oh, let me, Dad,' I whined. 'I'm not going to mess it up, am I? And I've got to do tons and I can't do anything with a biro. I'm completely stuck.'

'No way,' said Dad.

'Oh, let him,' said Mum. 'He's very good on the other computer ...'

'And it's rubbish, Mum, the one downstairs,' I said. 'It's really, really slow and it hasn't got Windows or anything.'

It took a bit of whingeing and please-oh-pleasing, but in the end, Dad gave in and said yes, I could use it – but only on condition that it stayed in his room, on his desk. 'And no drinks,' he said. 'The downstairs PC has never properly recovered since you spilt Tizer all over it.'

The trouble with Mum and Dad's bedroom is, it's a useless place to work in. You have to walk miles every time you fancy a biscuit or you need to make a quick check to see what's on telly. And Dad's desk is right in front of the window overlooking the garden – so you have to watch Sal and her little friend Tom on the patio spitting on ants and listen to them screaming their heads off. I wouldn't have minded so much if they'd managed to score one hit – but they used up all their spit and never even got close, as far as I could see. It was really frustrating, so I decided to go downstairs and shift them.

When I say shift them, I don't actually mean tell them to go away or anything. That's always a complete waste of time, 'specially with Sal. What I had to do was be dead cunning. I knew Sniff was curled up in the space behind the curtains in the sitting-room. He always goes there when it's hot. So I said, 'You mustn't go in the kitchen and play Doctors and Nurses, because you'll disturb poor Sniffy. He's lying down quietly in the sitting-room, OK?'

Sal said, 'Shaddup Bumbum' and started whispering to little Tom.

I nipped back upstairs and looked out of Mum and Dad's window. Brill! Telling Sal not to do something gets her doing it every time. Result – nothing on the patio but peace and quiet. I rubbed my hands together, banged my chest like Tarzan, selected an extra large font, pressed the CAPS LOCK button, selected 'Underline' and typed BEGINNINGS. Wicked! Dead impressive. Piece of cake on this machine.

The trouble with BEGINNINGS was that the only thing I could think to do for twenty minutes was write my name and the day I was born. Then it took me another twenty minutes to write:

'The hospital was one of the cleanest and

most hygienic they had in those days. Unfortunately, I was premature and came out sideways. I was just about the size of a satsuma and I had to spend three weeks in a ventilator in Intensive Care. The doctor said it was a miracle and all the nurses had a whip-round and collected me a whole sweet jar full of smelly rubber . . .'

Wicked! I thought. Old Cleggy's going to love this. Then I sort of found myself getting claustrophobic, stuck in that room all by myself with nobody to appreciate me. I started thinking how great it would be if I took a chair out into the front garden and carried on with the laptop on my lap! After all, that's where laptops are supposed to be, not on boring old desks in your parents' bedroom. Then all the people going past would see me working, and they would probably think – 'Cor, look at young Ben Moore. He must be dead clever, working with a flash PC like that.'

So I disconnected the laptop from the mains and from its printer and sneaked downstairs. I heard Sal and Tom talking in the kitchen and peeped through the crack in the door.

SAL: Hello Mister Doctor. Have you dot a doff?

TOM: Cough cough

SAL: Dink you megsin. *(Squeezes drop of Fairy Liquid into Tom's hand.)*

TOM: Woss dat?

SAL: Dass megsin. Dink it up. Snice.

TOM: Glug glug. Yuck! *(Spit spit.)*

Pathetic really, but they were enjoying themselves in their little kiddy way. I grabbed a chair from the hall and was through the front door without them even having a clue what I was up to. Superior intelligence, that's all it takes.

It's amazing how boring the people in our road are, because hardly anybody went by. OK, Miss Morris from next door went past, but she didn't take any real interest, even though I started humming quite loudly to

myself so she'd know I was there. She went beetling on, obviously thinking it was sinful, me slaving away on a Sunday, so that was a waste of time. A couple of minutes after that, I heard footsteps, a man's judging by the sound, and I was just getting myself placed so that he could get a really good view of my ace word-processing skills – when there was this RAAALPH! RAAALPH! YIKE YIKE! from round the front of the house followed by screams and yells from Sal and Tom.

I guessed what had happened. By the sound of it, Sal must have got fed up with giving Tom injections with Mum's icing set, and decided to operate on Sniff's tail with the nutcrackers or something. They were all making such a racket that I knew I had to get back to Dad's desk megaquick before he came pounding up the path and twigged I'd been outside with his precious machine. I couldn't risk him seeing me with it so I grabbed the laptop and stuck it out of sight under a bush by the fence, then legged round to the side passage. I shinned up the wisteria on to the garage roof, then up the drainpipe into the bathroom window. Once I was in, it only took a sec to dive into Mum and Dad's room and get into position behind the desk. 'And all because the little lady loves being a pain,' I panted to myself.

Just as well I'm so amazingly athletic, because it was chaos out the back. I was wrong about the nutcrackers but right about the tail. Doctor and Nursie had bandaged it up nicely in kitchen foil. Sniff apparently thought the aliens were after him and he was spinning round on the lawn like a washing machine on final rinse, trying to shake them off. Doctor and Nursie had got over-excited and were dancing about, taking it in turns to shove each other off the patio. Mum and Dad were going bananas trying to figure out some way of interrupting Sniff in mid-cycle. Dad glanced up and saw me through his bedroom window apparently working away quietly at the laptop. 'Don't just sit there like a pudding!' he yelled. 'Get down here and do something, boy!'

I zoomed downstairs and out on to the patio, arriving just in time to see the foil shoot off. Sniff staggered to a stop, fell over, and then decided it was time he shot off himself . . . which he did. He tottered away towards the front garden, afraid that his escape route to the Rec via the loose board in the back fence was cut off by Mum and Dad.

I whizzed after him calling Doggy Chocs, but he was far too upset to concentrate. There were only two things that he wanted just at that moment: one was a nice mad run at full revs round the neighbourhood. The other was a good pee – which he was in the middle of, I discovered, as I arrived in the front garden. He must have been saving it up for hours, because it went on and on like a garden sprinkler. And just my luck – he was aiming it at the bush by the fence. I  might have got away with it if Sal hadn't blabbed about me having a go at the laptop with Mum's hairdrier.

Some people I know – Thurston for one – try to blank out all the really painful times in their life. But I remembered Cleggy telling us how great writers have a knack of turning their suffering into art. So I shut myself in my room, got out a new sheet of paper, picked up my biro, pulled out the little plug with my teeth and, just like that, the title suddenly popped into my head: THE MISUNDER-STOOD YEARS.

Then it all started to flow.

# Sniff the Hamburglar

You could tell by the strain on Dad's face that Mum's rubber gloves were two sizes too small. And, I didn't like to mention that they were the one she uses to clean the toilet, because he hates peeling vegetables.

It was a wicked Sunday morning – really sunny and everything. All you wanted to do on a day like that was to be outside, putting a new alternator on the car. Only Mum had the car.

Me and Dad were lumbered in the kitchen.

'Shall I go down the corner shop and get you some sherbet lemons?' I said, thinking it might cheer him up a bit, but he just told me to get knotted and find the saucepans for him.

'Why do I have to suffer as well?' I grumbled.

'We are not suffering, Ben,' he said. 'We are supporting your mother. You know how important this second-hand pine furniture idea is to her. And we shall be the ones to reap the benefit when she starts making money. The least we can do is prepare the Sunday lunch while she's round at Bunty's doing a deal with Vincent. If they can get him to move the stuff in his van at the right price, they're in business.' He almost sounded convinced.

'I hate Vincent,' I said. 'He thinks he's so cool.' Vincent is this corny, pasty-faced old hippy with a pony tail who hangs around the market and auction rooms in Bridge Street. Just because he dropped out of Mum's university, he thinks it's OK to keep coming round our house and witter on about plate racks and wardrobes.

'He's quite a character, Vincent,' Dad said

bitterly, and jabbed away at the spuds. I think he was a bit jealous.

'I don't know why you let her go out with him, Dad,' I said. 'He is so sad. He's got green teeth, have you noticed?'

'Do shut up, Ben,' Dad said. 'You're talking nonsense. They are not going out. They are discussing business.'

'And it's all right for Bunty,' I said, banging cupboard doors open and shut. (How was I supposed to know where Mum kept the saucepans?) 'She's got more muscles than you have. She's not going to have any probs stripping sideboards and all that, but what about Mum? She's only small.'

'Don't you believe it, old son,' Dad said. He hacked another great chunk off the spud he was doing, which left him holding a thing the size of a pea. He flipped it in the direction of the colander and missed. It bounced off the floor and rolled under the dishwasher. 'Your mother's tough as old boots. Remember how she ripped out the fireplace in the sitting-room while I was away on that course in Swansea? Get that spud, will you?'

'Yeah, but that was only because you said there was no way anybody could budge it,' I reminded him, really cheesed off at having to look for two things. Dad just nodded at that, then he grabbed a carrot and had a real whittle at it, like he was trying to sharpen a tent pole or something. He kept whittling till he was holding this thing that looked like the stub of an orange pencil.

'D'you want me to do the carrots, Dad?' I suggested – only because I could see we were all going to starve if I didn't do something drastic.

'Reverse psychology, Ben,' he said. 'You're right.'

'What's that supposed to mean?' I said.

'Look, son, you've sussed what happened about the fireplace,' he said. 'I only told your Mum no way is anybody going to be able to shift that fireplace – because I knew she'd see it as a challenge ...' He slid his gogs back up his nose and left a strip of carrot skin on the frame. 'So we might as well think about what is going on here, OK? Pay attention. Now, number one. Do we want the place stinking of methylated spirits and varnish? No. Number two. Do we want a load of old chairs and tables and blanket chests in the garage?'

'No,' I said. 'There're piles of junk in there already.'

'Exactly!' he said. 'Important junk! Essential junk! So how are we going to get anything done in this house if your mother starts stripping furniture in there? How are we going to get at the tools and put the car away and everything? The garage is a vital space for us, right? So how do we hang on to it . . . ?'

'Reverse psychology!' I said. 'I get it! We encourage her to go into the furniture business and she'll pack it in.' So that was what this was all about!

Dad was whistling I Did it My Way when Sniff dragged in a baked ham.

'It's a work of art!' said Dad. 'And it must weigh seven or eight pounds at least.'

Sniff sat patiently on the kitchen tiles, long drooly strings hanging out of the corners of his mouth. Every now and then he rippled like a washing machine doing its final spin. Maybe he thought Dad was going to carve it for him. Dad put it on a big serving plate on the kitchen table and examined it closely, rolling it over. 'It's beautifully glazed,' he said. 'And look at the way it's been studded with cloves. Magnificent! And it smells – mmmm – delicious!'

'There're no marks on it, Dad,' I said. 'Few bits of grass, that's all. Be a shame to waste it – and I'm fed up with chicken anyway.'

'Forget it,' Dad said. 'It's one thing Sniff bringing in dead seagulls and dried cowpats and stuff. But it's quite another thing when he waltzes in here with somebody's Sunday lunch. We've got to do something about this. We've got to act responsibly here, Ben – especially as it's very likely somebody saw him fetch it in here. So the first thing is . . . stick this in the fridge until we work out whose it is. Open the door for me, old son.'

As soon as it was safely out of Sniff's way, he stood by the sink for a mo, thoughtfully wiping his hands on the curtains, while the old eager look came into his eyes. 'Which way did Sniff come – across the Rec and through the back? Or from the road?'

'No idea,' I said. 'I was looking for the saucepans and the spud you dropped – remember?' I shoved this huge great pan with two handles into his hands. There was nothing in it – only a pea-sized potato with a bit of fluff on it – but it weighed a ton.

Dad started loading the pan with veg from the muddy water in the sink, most of it unpeeled, while he was thinking what to do. Finally he said, 'Right. I've got it. We'll put the chicken in the oven, put the veg on – might as well bung them all in this pan – it's big enough. Then we'll take a quick look round the neighbourhood – see if anybody looks as though somebody just swiped their lunch.'

'What are they going to do, Dad – put a sign up? "LOST. ONE VERY NICE GLAZED HAM. ONLY GOT ONE LEG. ANSWERS TO

THE NAME OF PORKY"?'

'Lowest form of wit, sarcasm,' said Dad, donking me on the top of the head with the loaded pan on his way to the gas stove.

'Yow!' I said. 'That's dangerous, Dad!'

'Stop moaning and set the oven for the chicken,' said Dad. 'What's the top temperature on the regulo thingy?'

'280 degrees,' I read, still checking my skull for fractures.

'Just the job,' said Dad. 'That should kill all the salmonella bugs, anyway. You can't be too careful with chickens these days.'

'Shouldn't we take the little plastic bag out?'

'Let's have a look,' he said and squinted up the poor thing's bum. 'No, that's to keep the juices in or something, I expect. Slap a dollop of butter on its chest and bung it in. We've got to get cracking. Your mother'll be back in an hour or so.'

Dad decided that the most important thing to do first was to check the locals for signs of rage and frustration. After the business with Mrs Nicholson's pekinese bitch and the Greenaways moaning about Sniff burying the bread they put out for the birds, our doggy was not exactly flavour of the week.

We worked out – well, Dad did really – that, since the houses in our road back on to the playing fields, Sniff had most likely got into somebody's kitchen through their back fence. Even so, he reckoned we should look for signs of activity out the front – people searching under hedges, maybe, or getting a gang together to come and beat us up.

'We'll take the bikes, speed things along,' Dad said, meaning mine and Mum's. 'Then we just act natural. You go up towards Glebe Crescent and I'll go the other way.'

'But Dad, it's not going to look exactly natural if you go on a bike. You never ride a bike. Besides, Mum's has got a flat tyre,' I reminded him as we reached the shed. 'You said you'd fix it last week.'

'And what stopped you fixing it?' he snarled. 'Anyway – time's winged chariot hurrieth near and all that – so walking is out of the question. This will have to be a handlebar job.'

'Bags you handlebars, then,' I said. 'You're hopeless at steering.'

'I'm going saddle. You can pedal and steer – but just get a shift on,' he said and hopped towards the front gate, tucking a trouser leg in his sock at the same time. 'Efficiency,' he puffed and wiggled his eyebrows up and down while he swung the gate open.

'Yeah, yeah, the engineer's motto,' I said and pedalled out into the road.

I found it a bit wobbly at first with Dad on the back but there was no traffic so it didn't matter which side of the road we were on. 'You're doing all right, boy!' Dad yelled in my ear. You could tell he was enjoying himself. 'Now let's get this crate moving!'

I got my head down and went for it, heading Glebe Crescent way first. Everything had a real Sundayish feel at first, with nobody about, not even gardening or washing cars. 'Shall I turn back and try the other end, Dad?' I puffed.

'Why not go once round the Crescent?' said Dad. 'We could practise a nice co-ordinated lean on the corner.' He was really getting into it. We banked into the crescent and cruised round in a wicked curve. Still no sign of anybody, so Dad said to hit it again. In the end, we went round Glebe Crescent four times, getting better with every circuit. Third time round, a tall, fuzzy-haired bloke came out to his front gate to watch. Fourth time, another bloke was with him – tubby old guy with a moustache, wearing the sort of droopy cardigan that Aunt Cress knits. They waved us down.

'Oh, no,' I thought. 'Here we go.'

'Bob Moore, isn't it?' said the fuzzy bloke.

'And my son, Ben,' said Dad nervously.

Walked right into it, I thought, struggling to get my breath back.

'I'm Tim Wendling – and this is Charlie Henderson, my neighbour,' said Fuzzy. You could tell by the way he was picking his forefinger, he was having trouble finding words. 'Look, the fact is . . .' he said and fizzled out.

The tubby guy, Mr Henderson, licked his moustache. It was one of those moustaches Wing Commanders have in old war films about the Battle of Britain. 'Know you, don't I, Ben?' he wheezed. 'Helluva big hound you've got, am I right? Name of Sniff, I believe . . .'

I was thinking there was no way I could make a fast getaway with Dad on the back. I nodded.

'Had him long?' asked Mr Henderson, dead casual, twiddling his thumbs across his fat tum. Anyone could see it was a trap, so I just puffed and smiled and played for time. He looked like the kind of bloke who would really miss his Sunday lunch, if you know what I mean.

'One feels a bit of a clot asking you this,' broke in Mr Wendling, 'but we saw you thrashing round the Crescent just now . . . and it crossed our mind . . . Please say if this is out of order . . . but . . .'

'Look, no point in beating about the bush,' stammered Mr Henderson. 'You wouldn't by any chance . . .'

'. . . give us a go,' blurted out Mr Wendling.

So there I was, left to trace the owner of the missing lunch all on my own – while Dad and his new chums, Charlie and Tim, took it in turns to two-up round and round the Crescent on my bike.

'I say – keep an eye out for the law, you chaps – eh, what? Ha ha ha!' I heard Mr Henderson roaring as Dad wobbled dangerously off round the corner with Mr Wendling on the back, and I legged it down our road to check out the scene at the other end. So embarrassing when grown-up men get like that.

The only person I met in the road was Miss Norris from next door, on her way back from church. I thought I might as well check her out. 'Looking forward to your lunch?' I said, all friendly, as she went marching past. Big mistake. I should have just kept my head down like I normally do – because she stopped and looked at me as if I was taking the mickey.

'Well, Ben,' she said. 'I shall consume my sardines on toast with particular enthusiasm, knowing that your best wishes go with them. Good morning.'

Touchy or what? I thought as I cut down the path at the side of our house and made my way into the garden. But at least I'd found out that she hadn't invited the vicar for a nice slice of glazed ham. So the only thing now was for Sherlock Moore to hop over the back fence, get on to the Rec without drawing attention to myself and have a quick check on the action in one or two back gardens.

I had no joy with the first six or seven houses. I could see by just jumping up and sticking my head over the fence, or by just sneaking a look through the gaps that mostly everything was pretty normal with people lazing about, or yelling at their kids, or oiling their lawnmowers. Then when I got to the Marshes, I heard this machine going, making a sort of booming, moany noise. I was dying to see what was going on, but it took me ages because their fence is so high and somebody had been round with plastic wood and filled in all the knot-holes. They're like that, the Marshes. They think they're so perfect. Luckily, I remembered this periscope I'd made out of cereal packets that was in our shed. I got the idea off Blue Peter but I'd improved on their design by including a little mechanism for altering the angles of the mirrors. It was really ace, so I decided to nip back and have a look for it.

It took a bit of time, but it was worth it, and it finally turned up behind this box that was full of little bits that Sal must have hidden there – like the ears she'd cut off her teddy, and a stale French loaf with both points bitten off that Mum had blamed me for eating the weekend before. Sniff must have seen me going into the shed, and he sounded so miserable – you could hear him howling away in the living room – I couldn't leave him without giving him something to cheer him up. Good thing he's nuts about stale bread. All I had to do was slide the

French windows open a bit and bung in the loaf. That quietened him down straight away. He jumped on to the sofa and started giving it a good chew.

The periscope was a bit cobwebby and there were a couple of dead flies rattling around in it, but I soon managed to clean it up enough so that it was about eighty per cent efficient. So off I went again to check out the Marshes. There was a couple walking a poodle, way over the other side of the Rec near where the cabbage fields start, so I tried to look as unsuspicious as possible and just casually brought the periscope up to my eye as I sort of strolled past the Marshes' fence. I couldn't believe it! Mrs Marsh was vaccuming her patio! I thought of going back for my camera, so I could get a snap to show Thurston and Max. We saw her once, scrubbing bird-poo off her front gate with a toothbrush. Thurston had this ace idea of sending Mr Marsh a note warning him to check his bristles before he cleaned his teeth that night, but we chickened out of it.

Beep! My watch went off. One o'clock already! No time for photos when there was the Case of the Missing Baked Ham still to solve. Concentrate, concentrate!

The Barbers have got this really smart hedge round their back garden – yew, I think it is – all neatly clipped anyway, and dead thick, so they don't bother too much about the state of the fence, which has a huge big gap in it with three boards missing. You can crawl right in there and suss things out, no problem. It was the first time I'd had a proper look at the new conservatory they had, like something out of Kew Gardens – dead flash, actually. And in the middle of the conservatory, there was this mega table, with this wicked food on it, set out for eight people. It was a real feast, with big bowls of pasta, samosas, chick peas, kidney beans, Greek salad and potato salad, flans, pastry parcels – and piles of yummy things I'd never seen before. And guess what – right in the middle of the table, was this ginormous empty oval plate . . . BINGO!

It only took me about two minutes to nip home, grab the ham, wriggle my way under the Barber's hedge, sneak across their lawn, dive into the conservatory (the door was open to keep things cool, so I thought – Aha! this must have been how Sniff got in in the first place), and put the ham back on the plate. It was really scary, 'specially getting across the lawn both ways without being spotted, but I made it OK.

Soon I was safely back in our garden, panting like crazy and congratulating myself on being Mr Fixit. That was when I noticed Sniff all tangled up in the net curtains he'd pulled down behind the French windows in the living-room and the black smoke pouring out of the kitchen ventilator. I was thinking – Wait up. Black smoke . . . ? BLACK SMOKE!! WOW! . . . FIRE!!!

I started doing my write-up for the local paper as I was running for the back door.

'Heedless of his own safety, young, athletically-built Ben Moore braved dense smoke and terrible flames at his home on Sunday to rescue the family pet . . .'

Before I got there, somebody heaved it open from the inside.

'Get the oven door open!' yelled Bunty. 'And I'll blast it with the foam!'

'Maybe we should use the fire blanket!' shrieked Mum, coughing like mad.

'Don't worry! The electric's off. Give it a ruddy good dowsing!' boomed Bunty.

'I'll do it, Mum!' I yelled. I was dying to have a go with the fire extinguisher.

I don't remember exactly what Mum said but I got the idea she wasn't all that pleased with me, and I'd better just go round the front and keep Tom and Sal and myself out of the something way.

There was a horrible mess and – OK, so we'd made a couple of mistakes. I admit it wasn't a great idea to put a pan of veg on the stove and leave it to boil dry. But how was I supposed to know that Mum used that big pan to boil Sal's overnight nappies? God, we could have been poisoned! And how was I supposed to know that chickens incinerate after about half an hour at 280 degrees?

Things could have got very nasty if Dad hadn't turned up at the back door looking really hot and happy with his new chums – Mr Henderson and Mr Wendling.

'Hello, darling! Hello, Bunty!' he puffed, all jolly. 'Just brought Tim and Charlie round for a nice cooling drink. Pretty hot out there, actually, but a hell of a lot of fun riding two-up! And do you know – Tim here can do this trick where he sits on the handlebars and pedals at the same time . . . and CRIKEY! Looks like the Last Days of Pompeii in here!'

'There's been a slight accident, I'm afraid,' said Mum through gritted teeth. 'But don't let us interrupt you, darling, not if you chaps are enjoying yourselves.'

'Ah,' said Mr Henderson and Mr Wendling together, taking the hint. 'Um – we'd better be off.'

'Lunch calls,' said Mr Henderson.

'Yes, me too,' wheezed Mr Wendling, mopping his face with a large hankie. 'Must go and change. Wife and I've been invited to the Barbers. Big occasion, actually. They're celebrating their new conservatory. Should be a jolly good blow-out, eh? Ha ha!' He rubbed his hands and licked his lips nervously.

He had no idea how lucky he was that Sherlock Moore had been on the job. He could have starved if it wasn't for me.

'Didn't know you were a Veggy, Charlie,' laughed Mr Henderson.

'What d'you mean – "Veggy"?' said Mr Wendling.

'Nut roast for you, old man. Mrs Barber's President of the Southern Counties Vegetarian Society. Never lets a lamb chop darken her door! Not even her new conservatory door!'

I felt myself going green.

'Speaking of lunch,' said Bunty, poking Dad in the chest with a mighty index finger. 'Your blasted dog pinched ours off the top of the fridge while Jo and I were chatting to Vincent. At least, we're pretty sure it was him, aren't we, Jo?'

'Must have followed me and Sal round to Bunty's house,' Mum agreed. 'You haven't seen Sniff running about with a baked ham, have you?'

'A seven-and-a-half-pounder,' grieved Bunty. 'I'd glazed it myself. It took me hours.'

'Miff in na sitty room,' called Sal. 'He eatin sumfink.'

Everybody rushed to have a looked. Dad was looking the same colour as me.

'It's stale bread!' said Mum. 'He's got it all over the furniture. Still. No sign of your ham,

Bunty.'

Sniff's ears went up hopefully at the mention of the warm ham.

'It'll turn up somewhere, I'm sure,' said Mr Henderson, trying to look on the bright side.

'Yes, let's - er - hope so,' agreed Dad, trying to mime 'Where the heck is it?' to me without anybody else seeing.

'What - a baked ham? TURN UP?' Mr Wendling roared with laughter. 'Baked hams don't just turn up, old boy! I'm sorry, but that's ridiculous!'

He was still laughing as he set off to change for his lunch at the Barbers.

# Snapping with Sniff

I hate going to car boot sales with Mum. I bet they have car boot sales in Hell and you have to spend forever – with nothing to eat or drink – trailing after your Mum, your dog and your screamy little sister, looking at home-made earrings, second-hand plastic shower curtains, painted clogs, and knitted pot holders.

Dad was being a complete pain as well. He was after some prize at his Camera Club. They were having this show or something – so there he was, snapping away, squinting through his view-finder, knocking over brass knick knacks with his elbows, backing into people's dried flower displays, treading on their feet. Well embarrassing!

Then I had this brill idea of steering him towards the hot dog van by getting him to come and look at a whole load of old photographic junk in the back of the car parked next to it. Just my luck that Dad spotted this Ikelite underwater housing that he reckoned would fit his camera. Instead of a hot dog, I ended up with a long lecture on the nifty little gear wheels that connected the focus and exposure adjustments to the external controls and what an incredible bargain it was at only thirty-eight quid.

I tried to look fascinated, hoping that Dad would reward me with a Monster Dog with double onions and all the extras, or buy me this practically brand new pump-action air gun I'd just noticed that only cost fifty-five pounds, but he just told me to get knotted and made me run about four miles to the nearest chemist to buy a fast film for underwater photography.

When I got back, he was having a row with Mum. She said thirty-eight quid was a stupid price and he'd wasted his money.

'But darling, this kind of accessory costs a fortune in the shops!' Dad said, trying to get her interested in the underwater housing. 'Next to the cast aluminum ones, these Ikelite jobs are the best you can get. And it's just what I need to give me some really original shots for the Show.'

Mum ignored him and made a dive to stop Sal poking Sniff's eye out with a toasting fork she'd just pulled out of a nearby cardboard box.

Dad cheered up a bit when I put the fast film into his hand. 'Ah, thanks Ben! Great. ASA/1000. Should be able to work in considerably reduced light with this little beauty!' He whipped out the old film, put it under his arm, and started winding on the new one. He was all shaky with excitement. 'Now,' he said, 'we're all set to slip the camera into the housing. Just a question of lining it up correctly and . . . hmm . . . bit more fiddly than I thought.'

He squatted down, adjusted his gogs and

concentrated on his task. When he stuck his tongue out, he reminded you of Sal sitting on her potty, flicking through a rag book. 'And it's only got this one little mark on the front glass, darling,' he added, trying to suck up to Mum. 'Otherwise it's in perfect nick. What d'you think this little mark is, by the way ...?'

'Probably the blood of the last man to waste a fortune on the thing without consulting his wife,' said Mum, jabbing him up the bum with the toasting fork she'd just confiscated from Sal.

'Ouch! That's not funny, Joanna!' yelled Dad, jumping about ten feet. But Mum and Sal practically wet themselves laughing – well, Sal did wet herself laughing, actually – and, between them, they got Sniff going. He jumped on the used film that had dropped out from under Dad's arm, tossed it up in the air to scare it and gave it a good crunch to finish it off when it came down.

Twenty minutes later, we were parked near Felcombe pond. 'Well, don't come running to me if he dies of exposure,' tutted

Mum, just loudly enough to needle Dad without waking up Sal and Sniff who had both zizzed off in the back of the car.

'Yeah, Dad,' I agreed. 'This is insane.' It was freezing, standing in my boxer shorts, clutching Dad's camera now finally in its underwater housing. Besides, I thought it was safer not to let on to Mum that I was quite keen to find out if it really worked, not while she was still in her killer mood.

'Come on, son, be a sport. It's taken me half the afternoon to figure out how to fit the thing on to the camera. I'm not going to get any results from the film Sniff chewed, am I? So if I'm going to be able to hold my head up at the Camera Club, I need a bit of help. Think of it as taking part in a brief scientific experiment.' He pulled his shirt off over his head and there he was, naked except for his blue and white striped Marks and Sparks knickers, his legs and arms looking incredibly white and hairy and goose-pimply. 'Let's get in quick,' he said, 'before somebody comes. Wait till I get the face mask on, then pass me the camera and get in the pond.'

'But, Dad – look at all that green scum round the edge,' I shivered.

'You're not scared of a touch of duck poo, are you, boy?' he scoffed, wading in up to his knees and peering through the view-finder of the crazy piece of junk that had started all this. 'Brace up a bit, Ben. When you see the results, you're going to be delighted you got involved in this venture. So, come on, now, this won't take a mo.'

'I know your "mo"s, Dad,' I said. 'Why don't you get Sniff to get in there for you?' I moaned. 'It looks freezing.' Even the massive great swans feeding by the steps over the other side of the water looked well chilled out.

'Oh, come on! Quick!' said Dad. 'That's enough spit to keep the face mask clear. Hand the camera over. And in you get, boy. Start over here, next to me, and try not to stir up the mud too much, OK?' We started wading towards the middle and I don't know which was worse, the feeling of slimy gunge squidging between your toes with every step – or the way the cold knocked the breath out of you.

'Don't rush anything,' Dad went on. 'Let's keep the water nice and clear. Now, I'll tell you what we're going to do. We're going to keep wading, taking it steadily until we get to the middle, so not far now. That's it. Never mind about the cold. With a bit of luck, you should be up to your neck in a minute and you won't notice it so much. Keep going. And what I want to do is – I want to get a couple of shots from underwater of you floating on the surface. That way, we get maximum light, 'specially if we wait till the sun comes out from behind the clouds.'

'Very interesting, Dad,' I said, through chattering teeth. 'But my main problem is that I think my legs have just dropped off.'

'Do brace up, Son,' said Dad, 'and concentrate while I show you how to take a picture, so you can do some after me.' He showed me how to hold it steady by pressing it against the face mask and where to put my trigger finger. 'The idea is to make the subject look interestingly distorted, you see, like some sort of creature from the depths,' Dad said. 'Because objects underwater seem to be at least a third bigger than they really are – that's a feature of refraction. Fascinating, eh?'

'Can we get on with it, Dad?' I begged.

He took a massive breath and ducked out of sight. I felt him tugging at my ankle and I took that to be the signal that I had to start posing. I didn't have a lot of choice and, even though the freezing water made your head feel like somebody was squeezing it in a vice, I stretched out and tried to make like the Loch Ness monster.

He popped up and said he was quite pleased but could I maybe put my face under and squeeze a few bubbles out of my nose this time. We tried that. But he was still worried about reduced angle of coverage or something, so off I had to go again.

It was about then that Sniff woke up. He jumped out of the car and hared off to the steps on the other side of the lake to introduce himself to the swans. The swans took one look at the four-legged nutcase galloping in their direction, his tongue streaming over his shoulder like a flag and decided not to stick around to say hello. They turned round, jumped up on to their toes and started bombing towards the middle of the lake, smacking the surface with their ginormous wings and screaming blue murder. I couldn't have moved faster if a lorry from Universal Studios had backed up and dropped Jaws into the water. I shot back on to the grass from where I'd started like squeezed tooth-paste.

Next thing I knew, Sal was poking a cornet in my ear, offering me a lick, and saying, 'Dat your one. I et thum ob it.'

'Thanks a bunch, Sal,' I shivered, waffling down what was left. Meanwhile, Dad was yelling at me to stop splashing because I was clouding the water and he'd have to take another shot.

'Dad, I'm over here!' I said, my mouth full of cornet.

'Watch out, darling! Those swans look a bit fierce!' called Mum, but Dad obviously had his ears full of duckweed or something. The other problem was that he'd had to take his gogs off to fit the face mask on.

'Hang on a sec, Ben,' he said short-sightedly to the nearest swan, 'I need a bit more spit on the old face mask. Misted up rather a lot, I'm afraid.'

'Darling!' Mum called again. 'I really think

you should come out. You could get hurt!'

'Don't fuss, babe,' said Dad. 'Just one more shot, eh Ben, then it's your go?' The swan he'd spoken to so confidently waited until Dad's blue and white striped knickers broke the surface as he duck-dived, and then struck like a cobra.

'Pity I didn't get a shot of that,' I said to Mum, but I don't think she heard me.

'Blast!' spluttered Dad, breaking the surface again. 'You made me forget to wind on, cracking me on the bottom like that. I got a magnificent shot of your feet, too, Ben. The distortion made them look like paddles almost – and now I've mucked it up . . . and Ben . . .'

'MIND DA WACK-WACKS!!!' screamed Sal. He heard that. So did Sniff. He came whizzing round our side of the lake, rrralphing like crazy. The swans didn't have time to break Dad's beak with their wings, or whatever it is swans do to you when they're angry. They skitted over the water, then stretched their wings and glided behind the cover of some bushes and out of harm's way.

Normally, when he turns on the little red working light in the dark room, no matter how terrible he's feeling, Dad starts to cheer up. That night, not even the nice cosy smell of the chemicals and the hum of the enlarger could get a smile out of him.

'How's it feeling, Dad?' I said, meaning his bruise. That wasn't too bright of me, because I should have remembered that Sal had made him show it to all her teddies, dollies, stuffed rabbits and Snoopies before she would go to sleep.

'It's not the pain. It's the humiliation,' he muttered. 'Your mother's never going to let me live this down. She's already phoned Aunt Cress about it so it'll probably be on the television news now. And I've got absolutely zilch to enter for the Camera Club Show. Look at this roll of film that Sniff chewed. Knackered.'

'Cheer up, Dad,' I said. 'Maybe it's only the cassette. Let's open it up and take a look.'

When we got the film out of the cassette,

we found that the tooth marks hadn't quite gone through to the end. The last few frames were sort of dented but not punctured. 'Might as well stick 'em in the developer,' sighed Dad, hopelessly.

By the time we'd got the usable ones in the stop-bath and realized that they were snaps of the back views of Sniff and Sal, Dad was just about ready to kill himself. All his artistic work – down the drain. 'There's still the fast film,' I reminded him. 'At least the waterproof housing didn't leak, we know that.'

'But I only took about four or five shots. They're pretty well bound to be useless. I might as well hang on and use the rest of the film up on some family snaps later – otherwise it'll be a terrible waste of money. As far as the exhibition goes – forget it! One way and another, Sniff's made a complete dog's breakfast of my photos.'

'I'll tell you what, Dad,' I said. 'I reckon he might just have done you proud.' And I told him my idea.

'Quite magnificent, Moore. Wonderful textures here – and what an original treatment! Your work is in a totally different league from the rest of this year's entries. It has reached new heights of artistic achievement for the club. Our heartiest congratulations.' That, coming from the President of the Camera Club, was something.

Dad stood there, looking a bit stressed out in his best suit and Christmas tie, nodding and smiling and blushing away in front of all the mad keen photography freaks among his lecturer mates and their families. We were all there, for the Private View of the show, joining in the applause as Dad accepted the winner's trophy, and nibbling little snacky things.

The President turned to the display screen that was reserved for the winner's work and there, under the general title The Other Side, were a series of tight close-ups of what you might call 'abstract' photography. With a bit of trimming to cut out the background, there were some excellent close-ups of Sniff's hairy legs, entitled 'The Enchanted

Forest'. The underwater one of me churning about trying to escape the swans was wicked and the one where Dad forgot to wind on turned out to be really ace, too. It had a swan's body, my legs and webbed feet. Most of the rest were shots taken in the bath – taken underwater from plughole level – of Sal's entire collection of ducks, frogs, tug-boats, etc. (My idea). And the photo that was the outright winner – the most artistic one of the lot, according to me and according to the judges as well – was displayed on a special screen, all by itself under the title 'Crash-landing on the Moon'.

'This is the most intriguing of all,' beamed the President. 'The contours here, around the four smaller craters, are extraordinary – and I love the contrasting blacks and greys here, by the space craft in the main crater. Sensational technique. Exceptional power. I don't suppose you're going to let us into the secret ...?'

Of course, the 'space craft' was really only the mark on the glass front of an underwater camera housing, but he wasn't to know that. How could he? How could he know that the surface of 'the moon' started out as a close-up of Dad bending over in his Y-fronts, artistically captured in the prizewinner's bathroom by his incredibly brilliant son.

'Let's just say, I couldn't have done it without some help from my family,' said Dad, modestly.

'What, even the dog?' smiled the President, looking at Sniff who was drooling hopefully by a plateful of nibbles.

'One of my main artistic influences,' said Dad. He glanced round at the rest of the exhibits – most of which seemed to be pictures of old miseries in shell suits flogging junk out of the backs of Y-reg Datsuns – and slipped Sniff a handful of stuffed olives, cheese squares, cocktail onions and weeny sausages. 'He has wonderful taste, our Sniff.'

'Schloppp!' went Sniff, just to prove it.

# Sniff and the Binbag

Snow – the real thing and loads of it! So what was I doing wasting time just looking at it out of my bedroom window? I rolled over on the bed and stuck a hopeful arm underneath, feeling for my cold weather stuff. Monopoly box. Bits of Lego troop carrier. Fluff. Busted Airfix model of World War 2 Lancaster bomber (Dad's). Bunch of old computer games. Fat hairy head.

'Oh, come out of there, Sniff!' I moaned as he schlopped my face with his hot sticky tongue. 'I'm in a hurry and if you've chewed my moonboots, you're dead.'

To think I might have wasted half an hour's sledging time. Not that I had a sledge.

But I knew a little nerd who had.

'Bit brown, isn't it?' yawned Thurston into the phone. He was talking about the view from his bedroom window on his personal phone.

'Come on, Thurston, that is a definite covering of snow! It's centimetres thick! That is a blanket, man – and we should be out there. Have you got your gogs on, or what?'

'If you weren't a slab of fossiliferous oolite,' said Thurston, 'you would watch how to speak to me at this time of the morning. I don't have to go tobogganing, you know. I may just stay in bed and watch TV.' I heard him turn it on.

Thurston had this proper American 2-seater toboggan made out of polished wood like you get in films about places where it's snowing all the time and you always have to carry loads of thunderflashes just in case a polar bear pops out and tries to bite your arms off. Thurston's Dad brought it back from a business trip to Denver two years ago. We'd had a few pretend goes on it in his garage, but this was the first time we'd had a chance to try it for real on some decent snow.

'Oh, come on, Thurston, be a sport,' I said.

'Conditions are not ideal,' he said, turning up his telly.

'What do you want – icebergs?' I yelled.

'I want you to beg me,' he said.

God, that kid really knows how to annoy people.

Half an hour later me, Thurston and Sniff were steaming up what they call Gantry Hill on the common, just below the golf course, and the snow was still coming down – OK not much, but some anyway. Thurston was looking well hot and knackered, which was not surprising, since he insisted on dragging the sledge all by himself and it had this mega black binbag strapped to it, bulging with what he called 'survival gear'. I knew part of it was a complete change of clothes in case he got a bit damp but he wouldn't say what else there was.

The common looked well good, even if it

wasn't quite white all over, especially under the trees, and there was a bit of brown showing through where the early kids had scuffed it up. When I say early, I mean early, because it wasn't ten o'clock yet.

'God, you'd think they'd all be at home watching Rude Dog and the Dweebs,' panted Thurston scornfully, squinting up towards the track at the top where five or six kids in padded jackets and bright woolly hats were dotted about, chucking snow at one another and screaming their heads off. There wasn't much sign of sledging.

'What programme's that on?' I puffed but then I realized he'd got me again. He was talking about watching UK Gold or some other cable or satellite programme, knowing that I had to put up with just ordinary TV because my mum and dad think practically anything except BBC2 is environmentally unfriendly.

I reached up and twanged the branch we were ducking under. Thwaaaak! Thurston didn't have a chance to get out into the open, what with dragging the sledge behind him, so he got well splattered. A great glob of snow right down the neck! 'Eat that, sucker!' I yelled in my best Mr T voice, and ran for it.

The only trouble was, Sniff got all worked up when he saw me mucking about. He came whizzing towards me at full speed, did a flying drop kick, caught me off balance and sent me crashing back down the slope like an avalanche. When I finally stopped rolling over and over, he charged at me, spraying mud and snow like a bulldozer, grabbed my scarf and tried to shake it to death. He nearly killed me at the same time, dragging me about five metres on my face before I managed to unwind myself and let him run off with it. When I stood up, I looked like a cross between Frosty the Snowman and The Thing From the Swamp.

'Thanks, Sniff!' yelled Thurston, nearly wetting himself laughing. 'Saved me the trouble of taking my revenge!'

'You and whose army?' I spluttered, spitting out bits of leaf and muddy grass, and doing my best to skid back up the slope so that I could kill the cocky little dweeb. Sniff was nearly at the top of the track where the other kids were. You could see him, like a smudgy black ink-blot, chugging up the steepest bit of the hill, trailing my scarf after him, huffing out breath like a steam tractor at an engine rally. Before he reached the kids, he dropped the scarf, bounced back, spread his front legs and dropped down flat with a Rrrraaalph! that echoed all around the common. If he thought I was going to bother to chase him for it, he had another think coming.

'Get that dog out of the way!' bawled a posh voice. And then a kid suddenly materialized over the brow of the hill, belly down on his sledge and really motoring. Well, really motoring for a complete derr – because it turned out the kid was Ashley. I didn't recognize him at first, without his purple Quentin Court school blazer and prefect's badge.

'Look out, Sniff!' I yelled. He jumped to his feet, grabbed my scarf and started pretending he was having a death-struggle with a boa-constrictor.

'Sniff!' I screamed as Ashley thundered out of control straight at him. 'Shift yourself!'

To tell you the truth, I wasn't really all that worried, because people are always trying to run Sniff over but there's no way they can get him to stay still for long enough. Ashley wasn't to know that, though, was he? And seeing as he couldn't actually put any brakes on, the only thing he could do was chuck himself sideways and hope for the best.

Boy, you should have seen him roll! I thought for a second he was going to get down as far as me and take me out like a bowling ball – but he ran out of steam just about a metre short of where I was standing.

'Good one, Ash,' I said. 'Pity I didn't bring a camcorder. That one would have looked great on You've Been Framed, specially in slow motion.'

'Spectaculozoic!' agreed Thurston. 'And you look almost as grungy as Ben!'

'I could sue you, Moore!' Ashley moaned,

brushing muck off his shoulders and knees. 'You want to contwol that dog! I could have killed myself then!'

'That's a laugh!' piped up Thurston, who can never stay out of a good argument. 'You could have killed the dog, more like! You haven't even grasped the basic principles of tobogganing!'

'Yeah,' I added, getting into it – but I didn't get a chance to get any further, because Sniff, who had forgotten about my scarf, had gone skidding off after Ashley's runaway red plastic sledge and now he'd got hold of it. Ashley caught sight of him just as he started worrying it good and proper. 'Geddimoffitt!' he screamed.

'It's only plastic,' I said. 'He can't hurt it.'

'What do you mean plastic! That is polyvinyl chlowide.'

'Nothing special about PVC. Same stuff they make drainpipes out of,' sneered Thurston.

'Yeah, well I'll have you know that the Snowskimmer is a state-of-the-art sport-sledge, aewodynamically contoured in Norway to produce maximum thwust and minimum dwag,' fumed Ashley. He'd obviously memorized the label, but he looked dead chuffed with himself and straightened his bobble hat to make sure we could all see the last Winter Olympics logo on it. 'And if that . . . that . . . cweature of yours has left teethmarks in it, it's going to cost you a hell of a lot of money!'

I managed to trick Sniff by wiggling my scarf at him and grabbing Ashley's tow-rope at the same time. It was a bit soggy and chewed but no big deal. By now, the kids who had been mucking about at the top of the hill had heard the racket and come down to see what was going on. Andy, Chris Wormold and his brother Nevin were there – and some girl, wearing an 'I Heart Sydney' track-suit. She was tall and boney, with red sticky-out ears shining like brake-lights under her cropped fair hair.

'Neat slidge!' she said. She seemed really impressed by Thurston's toboggan.

'My cousin from Austwalia – Pansy,' said Ashley, knowing we hadn't seen her before. 'Her mother's visiting pwofessor of plant bio-chemistry to the University of London, so let's have some wespect fwom you two peas-ants.'

Thurston's eyebrows went up about a mile. 'What's her specialization?'

'Toxicology,' said Pansy. 'You know – poisons and all that.'

I happened to know that Thurston's secret ambition – when it wasn't to be a Top Chemist or a Top Geologist – was to be boss of the National Poisons Unit at Guys Hospital, so toxicology was one of his favourite ologies. Maybe that was why he suddenly got this look on his face like Sniff spotting Sunday lunch. 'Wow,' he said.

'That's a two-y, isn't it?' Pansy said, pointing at the toboggan. 'Why don't you and me give Ash a rice – down to that oak tree there?' When she pointed, you noticed how big her hands were. With hands like that, she could have scrunched Thurston like a crisp packet, but even if she looked like Bobby in Home and Away, it wouldn't have made any difference to Thurston ... if her mother was a poisons expert, he was in love – end of story.

'A race?' Thurston suddenly looked dead embarrassed, 'Yes ... well ... not exactly ... right conditions ... er, snow-wise.' For once in his life, he seemed stuck for words. 'Be delighted to give you a rice – race – ride, I mean ... but you need packed snow ... ice actually ... quite honestly ...' He burbled to a stop. It was definitely love. Yuck.

'Admit it,' said Ashley, taking advantage, 'it's a wubbish sledge.'

'Toboggan!' snapped Thurston. 'Genuine traditional American Indian winter transport. Go away and give me a chance to sharpen up my technique and we'll see what's rubbish.'

'Why should we?' said Ashley. 'We were here first.'

'Because I haven't even had one solo go on it yet, let alone a two-up. I need some time to work with Ben so that I can perfect my technique.'

'Fair go,' smiled Pansy. 'We can buzz off for a bit and check out the slopes over the other side of the golf course. That way you can practise, Ash, and so can … what's yer name, mate?'

'Thurston,' squirmed Thurston.

'Really? Never heard that one before. That's cute,' said Pansy. Thurston was lapping it up. It was pathetic. Then she said, 'Right, Ash, let's go and give these guys some space. Wouldn't be right otherwise.'

'Well, I shall thwash him anyway,' said Ashley. He pressed a button on his flash skin-diver's watch. 'Thirty minutes, Wilder.'

'Pretentious twit,' muttered Thurston as he unloaded his binbag full of supplies and dumped it on a spot where it couldn't run away downhill. Andy, Chris, Nevin and the rest disappeared over the other side of the hill with Ashley and Pansy. You could hear Nevin and Andy blowing a raspberry-version of Here we go-Here we go-Here we go.

And OK, I admit I did say to Thurston, 'All set, Cutey?' but only for a joke. He didn't have to punch me on the head.

What a bummer that toboggan turned out to be! Our first few practice rides were sad. With the two of us on it, it was like ploughing. Our weight just pressed the steel-reinforced runners right through the thin layer of snow and on to the grass, so we hardly got up any speed. It would have been quicker to walk but I didn't say anything to Thurston in case he got vicious again.

'Pity we haven't got a drop of bear grease,' sighed Thurston. 'That's how they lubricate the runners in the Frozen North.'

'Needs something,' I muttered. I was thinking – serves him right for going all gooey over some toxic Australian professor's daughter. Then I thought, God, if Ashley wins, neither of us will ever hear the end of it. This was getting humiliating, not only for Thurston but for me, being his mate and everything. Then it hit me. BINNNNGGG! Dog power. Obvious, really.

'Why don't we get Sniff to pull us?' I said. 'There's nothing in the rules that says you just have to rely on gravity, is there?'

'What rules?' said Thurston, suddenly much more chirpy and giving his steamy gogs a quick polish. 'Let's get sorted!'

'We'll get him to grab my scarf and just hang on,' I said confidently. 'Didn't you see the way he dragged me with it just now?'

But it was one thing to get him to drag you when the scarf was round your neck and something else when you were holding it and sitting on a toboggan. After a couple of shakes and a bit of a growl, he lost interest and started whizzing round in circles, trying to bite something on his bum.

'Give us your jacket!' I said, but Thurston wouldn't. 'Well give us your spare one, then,' I said. 'Only hurry up, we haven't got that much time.' Thurston undid the binbag and tipped a load of ski clobber on to the ground. I grabbed a quilted jacket, quite short in the arms – just the job. 'Here, boy!' I said. 'Here, Sniff!'

Sniff stopped chasing himself and backed off, looking all suspicious. 'Haven't got any food, have you?' I said to Thurston. 'He won't come otherwise.'

It turned out that in the bottom of the sack there was this ginormous picnic that Thurston's mum had packed for him because her little darling had missed his breakfast. There was a flask of hot chocolate and piles of cakes and biscuits and sandwiches all done up in tupperware boxes – loads of stuff. No wonder it weighed a ton! Typical. And trust him to keep quiet about it in case he had to share any.

One sniff of a Jaffa cake and Sniff was drooling down my moonboots. I let him have a couple, then I grabbed him, threw the quilted jacket over his shoulders and wrestled his front legs through the armholes. Zipping it up was a bit of a prob – with Sniff going mad, growling, trying to roll over and give me a good nip at the same time but I finally managed it. The plan after that was to tie Thurston's scarf and mine together and make a line from the sledge that would loop under the back of the jacket Sniff had on, so he wouldn't strangle when he started pulling. And why was he going to pull? This was the nifty bit. Thurston got this long stick and tied a sausage sandwich to it with the lace from one of his spare trainers. He was going to dangle it just in front of his nose and MUSH! – off we would go like White Fang.

That was the theory.

'Mush!' I said, as soon as Thurston was in a good racing position on the toboggan with the sausage sarnie dangling down as planned. Sniff looked at it. He sniffed at it.

Then he started to whine. Then he lay down, all shivery, and rolled his eyes.

'Wiggle it about a bit and say mush,' I said to Thurston.

'Mush is right. That's his brain, that is,' said Thurston. 'This is hopeless. He's far too stupid for this.'

'Right!' I said. 'That's it. Get off. I'll show you how to do it!' I snatched the sarnie-stick and gave him a shove.

'Oy!' screamed Thurston, as he went flying into the snow. I tried to dive on to the toboggan but Sniff suddenly whipped it away from under me and I fell flat on my face alongside Thurston. Next thing I knew, Sniff was off uphill yiking away with the toboggan bouncing after him like some crazy speedboat. He got about thirty metres above us before the scarves came undone and he went pounding off, jumping and dancing, trying to shake off the ski jacket.

Thurston and I were too busy trying to stop the runaway toboggan and avoid getting out teeth knocked out, as it came fizzing

down towards us, to notice that Sniff was
crawling into the empty binbag in search of
something tasty at the bottom. First thing we
know about it, there's this howl –
RRRROOOOOooooooo! – and this black thing
is streaking past us at a zillion miles an hour.
It was down by the oak tree in two seconds
flat.

'What was that?!!!' said Thurston. He
couldn't believe it.

Down by the oak tree, Sniff backed out of the binbag – a bit shaky, but with the old tail going like crazy. 'I think he wants another go,' I said.

It was obvious from the way Thurston's mouth was making wahwahwahwah shapes that even he was impressed. 'That's it!' he yelled, going into one of his hyper war dances. 'Polymethyl-methacrylate!'

'Wash your mouth out, Wilder,' I said.

'It's a device to reduce friction,' Thurston was explaining to Pansy who wasn't too keen to get on the back of something that looked like it had been put out for the dustman. She, Ashley and the gang had come back for the race to find that Thurston had stuck his toboggan into a binbag – well, a double one, actually, since his mother had supplied him with half a dozen spares as part of his survival gear.

'Does it go?' she asked anxiously. 'It looks really stupid.'

'Go? You don't want to judge by looks. It's been brilliant in trials, hasn't it, Ben?' said

Thurston. It was true, it went much quicker in the binbag, even with two up. 'The idea of reducing drag on the runners with a layer of polymethyl-methacrylate just came to me out of the blue. Quite simple – but incredibly effective as simple ideas often are. Hop on – you'll see.'

'I'll kill him,' I thought. I was really cheesed off. Not only was a girl being substituted for me in the big race, but now I was having to listen to him pinching the credit from my dog! 'Right,' I thought.

'Pwoper place for wubbish, a wubbish bag!' Ashley jeered and all the other kids who were set to give him a good shove-off from the starting line went 'Good one, Ash!'

'Huwwy up, you two,' he yelled. 'Let's get on with the wace! Who's starter? Moore?'

'Not me, I'm racing,' I said, shaking out one of the spare binbags and cutting a slit in the end with my penknife. 'Andy or Chris can be starter.' I pulled the bag over my head like a dress, stuck my head out of the slit and got down on the starting line on my belly. 'Give us a shove, somebody,' I yelled.

'Get stuffed,' said Andy and Niven together, but suddenly – galloping sounds – RUCK-ADDA DUKKADA DUKKADA – and there was this great squirmy thing, whining and panting with excitement, flopping down on top of me. 'MARKS-SET-GO!' I screamed because there was no going back now. A fat hairy head rested itself on mine and SCCHH-HOOOOM! – me and Sniff went down that hill like somebody had squeezed an orange pip!

'WICKED ride!' I yelled as I fizzed past the oak tree. The other two sledges were neck and neck and miles behind.

'Cheat!' screamed Ashley.

'False start!' screamed Thurston.

Sniff and I had time to get out of our bin-bag and start heading back up to the starting line before they shushed past us. I couldn't have cared less who came second because – judging by the way Sniff was bouncing about, barking – he was as keen as I was to get back to the top and have another go.

Ashley and Thurston were still arguing about who was first past the oak tree and Ashley was going on about unfair plastic assistance when I heard Pansy close behind me, asking me if she could borrow my penknife so she could make a headhole for herself in one of the spare binbags. 'It looked so cool,' she said. 'I really have to try it.' Then she told me she was just crizy about my doggie and asked me if I trained Sniff myself. When she said he was the most fenTESTic mongrel she'd ever seen, I started to realise that maybe she wasn't a complete waste of space after all. Better than Thurston anyway. He'd ditched me for a girl and pinched an idea off my dog. He wasn't my flavour of the month right now.

'What does your mother reckon is the most poisonous thing you can get in this country?' I panted as we headed up the slope for another run. Snowballs started to splat in the snow all round us. God, Thurston was a terrible loser.

'Well, the arum lily's pretty bad,' she said.

'Most people call them lords and ladies – they've got bright orange berries in a cluster – right? You see them in the hedgerow in the late spring, early summer. They attack your mucus membranes, so you swell up and you can't breathe. Then there's hogweed, yew berries, laburnum . . . They'll all kill ya. Why? You into poison?'

'Thurston's birthday coming up soon,' I explained. 'Never too early to start thinking about presents, is it?'

# Sniff and the
# Fair Cops

Sniff and Sal were sharing a Fish MacNugget and large fries. Mum wasn't too pleased when she found them, seeing it was gone midnight, the central heating was off, and they were getting tomato sauce all over Sal's bedclothes.

Sal was standing in her cot clutching the red packet of fries and Sniff was under it, trying to get his fat head into the polystyrene burger box. There was torn paper everywhere.

'Where did they get them from?' Mum asked Dad. He was shivering, picking squashed chips out from between his bare toes and trying to stop his jimjams falling down all at the same time. 'You don't know anything about this, do you Ben?' she went on, turning to me.

'It's a bit cold, but it tastes OK,' I said, nibbling a bit of MacNugget I'd found under a Snoopy.

'Don't eat it, Ben. You don't know where it's been!' warned Dad. Sniff's long tongue came out and schlopped the squashed chip out of his hand.

'Quick, get those things away from Sal,' whispered Mum. 'They might be poisoned or anything!'

'Don't worry, Mum,' I said. 'She eats slugs and stuff like that, she'll be OK.'

'Go back to bed, Ben!' said Dad loudly. He had to be loud because Sal was well cheesed off to be interfered with when she was having such a good time.

'And take Sniff with you!' yelled Mum as I headed for the door.

I had to drag him but I got him out eventually. I decided to take him into my bedroom, even though I'd banned him recently because I wasn't sure whether it was him or Sal who'd chewed the mouse for my computer. I knew if I tried to shut him in the kitchen he'd kick up a fuss and burrow under the door or something. There was at least a chance he'd settle down with me.

At first he paced round and round and barked every time Sal screamed, but eventually, after loads of huffing and scratching and whining, he plonked himself down on the end of my bed, curled up and zizzed off.

I was well knackered at school the next day but I managed to squeeze in a bit of a kip during private reading. When I came round, I did a quick check for notes on my back and, sure enough, there were a couple stuck there. One said:

I AM A COMPLET NRED KICK ME

The spelling was a dead give-away. It was either Beggs or Rickie Lomax. When I turned to look, I saw Lomax pretending to take an intelligent interest in The Hobbit and I just knew it was him because he has trouble concentrating on anything trickier than Topsy and Tim. I got him between the eyes with an ink rubber and read the other note. It said:

WHILE YOU HERE DO SNORING LIE
I HAVE EATEN YOUR PORK PIE

Thurston! It had to be. He was sitting right next to me. What a low down rat! I dived for my bag and felt around. I knew exactly where I'd left the pie. It wasn't pork pie actually, it was a fidget pie, my favourite, but Thurston wasn't to know that. And I'd left it between the peanut butter and jam sarnies and the carrot cake. It was gone.

'Just a wind up,' said Thurston, pushing his gogs further up his snubby nose and jumping to his feet as the bell went for the end of morning school.

'Good one, eh?' called Max, over the sound of scraping chairs and chattering kids. He was two desks back, grinning all over his freckly face. Then he went Da-dah!! and pulled the pie out from under his jumper.

'Thanks a bunch,' I said. 'That's all I need – your fluff all over my lunch.' I grabbed it off

Max and gave him a quick dead-arm for being such a sad kid.

'Let's go and eat. I'm starving,' said Thurston.

We shoved our way through the crowds to the sandwich room and found a table. Thurston produced a plastic package with little compartments with different kinds of food tucked into them, all individually wrapped. The Executive Snack, the label said.

'Cor! Where d'you nick that from?' said Max.

'My dad has them supplied for his office,' said Thurston.

'They're specially designed for maximum nutritional value while providing a balanced diet.'

'I'll try some of that,' said Max, pointing at something sweet and sticky-looking.

'Don't be so predatory,' said Thurston. 'Eat your own.'

'That's easy for you to say,' grumbled Max. 'You don't have to put up with my mum's sandwiches. Look at this.' He lifted the top slice of one of the great wodges and showed us this revolting, mouldy yellow gunge. 'Gorgonzola and piccalilli,' he explained.

'Here you are,' I sighed and ripped off a bit of fidget pie for him. He took it and stuffed it in his face. He rolled his eyes, licked his lips, and put his hand out for more.

'You're as bad as Sniff, you are,' I said and that reminded me of what had kept us all awake. I told him and Thurston about him bringing home the McDonald's stuff.

'Where did he get it from?' Max asked.

'And how did he get out and back in again?' said Thurston.

'Sal must've let him out,' I said. 'She can get downstairs by herself and she knows how to open the French windows.'

'Yes, but she didn't just give him the money and say – "There you go, boy, fetch me a MacNugget and chips" – did she?' said Max.

'Maybe he just found it in a litter bin,' suggested Thurston. 'Yuck. How fetid!'

'What's fetid?' said Max.

'Your feet and your sandwiches,' said Thurston.

It happened again the following night. Well, nearly. It was a big Mac this time, with extra pickle. You could tell that because there were slices of pickle all over the living-room floor – pickle being about the only thing in the universe that neither Sal nor Sniff will eat.

They were both zonked out on the sofa, fast asleep, when Mum found them at seven o'clock next morning. It was the panicky way she ran back upstairs to get Dad that made me think there was something up, so suddenly all of us made a rush for the living-room.

'So Sal must've opened the French win-dows . . .' whispered Mum, tiptoeing among the bits of scattered food and rubbish. 'Look, they're not quite closed' She slid them along until the catch clicked.

Sniff went 'Nnn-nnn' and started pedalling his feet in his sleep. Sal rolled over and stuck her thumb in but didn't wake up.

'All the bits are here, including the bill,' said Dad, on his hands and knees, gathering together torn cardboard and chunks of polystyrene. 'And look. The bag is practically intact.'

'So . . . somehow . . . he managed to get hold of a complete meal,' said Mum.

'You mean, like he didn't find it in a litter bin, then?' I said.

'This is worrying,' said Dad.

'You mean it confirms what we were saying last night?' said Mum, going really pale.

'What?' I asked. 'What does it confirm? And Dad, you're kneeling on a slice of pickle.'

'Mum and I think Sniff may be going out mugging people,' Dad said. He nodded about ten times like he always does when he's trying to say something serious.

'Sniff! A mugger? Dad, you've got to be kidding!' I said.

'He's a big dog,' said Mum, shaking her head thoughtfully. What with her going shake-shake and Dad going nod-nod, you would have thought there was one of Dad's Buddy Holly records on. 'A lot of people ... well at night ... in the dark ... he could easily frighten a nervous person and ...'

'Mum, he wouldn't hurt a flea!' Sniff suddenly sat up and pounded away at his chest with his back paw. 'Well maybe a flea – but he wouldn't hurt a person,' I said.

'Well, he does chase motorbikes,' whimpered Mum.

'We must consider the possibility, son,' said Dad. 'This could be a serious matter.'

'We could have the police involved in a thing like this,' said Mum. 'Even if they don't come looking for us, I honestly think ...'

Dad finished off for her '... we shall have to turn him in.'

'Turn him in? Dad, you make it sound like LA Law or something. He's just a stupid dog, not a criminal.'

'Mugging's a criminal offence!' Mum was dead upset. Sniff was wide awake now. As Mum sat down to have a little cry and a nose-blow, he jumped off the sofa and put his head in her lap. 'What have you done?' she wailed, stroking back his ears. He looked up at her with innocent eyes and ate her wet tissue.

Dad and I came up with an ace plan. We decided not to let Mum in on it in case she started worrying. Dad was going to get her to spend the night in the spare room – so that she could catch up on lost sleep, that was the excuse. Then we would follow Sniff and find out who he was pinching the food from. You could tell that Dad was really turned on by the idea of a boys-only adventure. He started getting all excited about it, giving me little eyebrow-wiggles every time he passed me – or doing that rabbity-thing he does with his nose.

I had to go to bed quite early – but I kept most of my clothes on. Dad was going to come and wake me up if there was any action. We thought that if Sniff made a break for it, he was most likely to head for town through the loose board in the fence in the back garden and across the Recreation ground. The late-night McDonald's was out on the new by-pass and you could get there from a turning off the High Street. So Dad was going to follow Sniff that way, across the fields. He thought it was a bit dodgy for me to be chasing about the Rec in the dark, but that I would be OK if I biked along the roads which were well lit – round by Irvine Street and up Cherry Lane to the High Street – to head Sniff off, in case he came back that way.

As it happened, I was up before Dad woke me at twenty past midnight, because I heard the familiar thump-thump of Sal going down-stairs on her bum. I had my quilted jacket on before he'd opened my bedroom door and I was off down the road on my bike before he'd sneaked out the back through the kitchen.

The cold was really bad on the ears and made your eyes water but I soon warmed myself up, knowing that I had to get a shift on to catch up with Sniff and Dad who were taking the short cut. In less than five min-utes, I was belting along past the chemist's and the greengrocer's and leaning to take the corner into Gammon Road which cut through on to the by-pass. It felt really weird under the yellow sodium lights at that time of a Saturday night with only the odd passing car for company, weird but exciting.

I'm not sure how long I hung around outside McDonald's. All I know is that it was freezing squatting behind parked cars by the entrance doors, keeping an eye out for Sniff or Dad for what seemed a heck of a long time. Every now and then I had to straighten up and do a quick sprint to the fence and back, just to keep the circulation going. It's amazing how many customers there were, all acting like it was normal to be ordering loads of hot yummy grub in the middle of the night when most people had to be in bed. I was so busy being jealous of them that I never even heard the policeman come up behind me.

I don't know if he really believed that I wasn't interested in breaking and entering cars, but anyway he helped me to stick my bike in his van and drove me home. He thought it would be a good idea to have a chat with my parents. I didn't dare say anything about Sniff mugging people for their suppers in case he decided to have him locked up. Which meant I couldn't really say anything about Dad being on a surveillance mission. I didn't have much luck thinking up an explanation for Mum, either, because we were outside the house in about two minutes flat.

We couldn't park right outside the house because of the police van that was already parked there. I felt well sick to think that they'd sent somebody ahead to tell Mum that I'd been arrested.

Next door's bedroom curtains were twitching away. I wasn't sure whether to ignore them or give Miss Morris a wave as I headed down the front path like a pirate walking the plank. I was quite surprised when Dad opened the door, gave me a weak smile, shook hands with my policeman, showed us into the living room and started on the introductions.

My policeman (PC Hudson) already knew PC Stickley who was busy doing something on his knees down beside the sofa, but he didn't know Mum or Sal. PC Hudson seemed as puzzled as I was by the turn-out, but he said some nice friendly hellos. Then all of a sudden he realized whose great hairy tum-tum PC Stickley was busy tickling. He slapped his knees and whistled to get Sniff's attention. 'Hoy! What about a bit of fuss for your Uncle Ron, then!' he shouted. 'Come on, you great soft Nelly!'

Sniff went all wobbly, scrambled to his feet, and lolloped over to greet PC Hudson like a long-lost brother. He jumped up and let himself be danced round by the front paws, whimpering and yapping with pleasure.

It must have been two o'clock in the morning before we got to bed.

'What a lot of red faces,' I heard Mum say after she'd tucked Sal in.

'Well,' said Dad, laughing, 'who would have thought those two coppers had been feeding

Sniff down at the police station? There we were worrying about having a delinquent dog in the family and all the time it was the police who were spoiling him rotten! What a pair of softies!'

'What about you and Ben?' said Mum. 'You and your all-boys-together midnight adventure stuff. You're both completely barmy!'

'Not bad, is it?' Dad giggled. 'Father gets arrested on suspicion of intent to vandalize the cricket pavilion. Son gets nicked on suspicion of intent to steal from cars. And all the time the arch-criminal is shut in the spare room with you!'

'I can't believe you were so daft as to leave without checking to see if Sal had actually let him out,' she said.

'And you haven't told me what she was doing downstairs if it wasn't to let Sniff out,' said Dad.

'She only went downstairs to collect her Snoopy from the sitting-room,' said Mum. 'I'd washed it to get the sauce stains off it and left it on the radiator to dry.'

'Rrrralph!' said Sniff, jumping up, wanting a fuss.

'All right, all right!' laughed Mum, scratching his ears. 'Let's all go back to bed.'

# Sniff and the Kissmus Present

It was bad enough Sniff yowling outside in the hall, covered in mud and mouldy old ashes, and trying to eat his way through the door. We didn't need Max moaning on.

'Shuddup Max!' said me and Thurston and Bruno together. We were spread out on the sitting-room floor, trying to concentrate on painting fiddly bits on Warhammer characters. There was loads to do if we were ever going to get a really epic battle going that afternoon round at Ashley's. Ashley, Roy Charterhouse and Nigel Cedric, three nerds from Quentin Court (that well-known academy for rich thickos), had challenged our High Elf force against their Goblin horde.

We were trying to get a production line going, because what we needed was warriors – plenty of them – Swordmasters and Standard Bearers and Archers with swords, warhorns, lances, bows, the lot. Bruno had this ace idea going for quick-drying our army between colours: he took off his ginormous baseball boots and socks, wedged an entire Command Group between his toes and wiggled them in front of the radiator. Even Thurston thought that was a wicked idea.

Max wouldn't shut up. 'It's bad luck, it's bad luck!' he kept whingeing. 'If you leave your tree up on the thirteenth day of Christmas, it's worse'n bustin a mirror. You should've chucked it outside yesterday, the 5th of January. My mum took all our decorations down last week.'

'Yeah, well your momma's not whacha call a fun person,' murmured Bruno.

'We don't need luck, just thoughtful tactics and brainpower,' said Thurston. 'And a well-equipped army – so fingers out, you guys.'

Sniff tried biting off the door handle to get in, and when that didn't work, he went RAAALPH! and chucked himself against the door. It sounded like a bomb going off. A shower of brown pine needles hissed on to the floor from the straggly branches of the dead Christmas tree by the fireplace. It looked well sad without its lights and stuff on.

'Kloggbags!' screamed Thurston. 'That blasted dog's made me smudge red all over the Repeating Bolt Thrower! I knew it was a ludicrous idea to try to do the painting round at your house, Ben.'

'Take it easy now, Thirsty!' drawled Bruno. 'That's only a li'l ol dawg out there! The way you're actin' up, anybody'd think it was Gorrfang Ratbreath's Goblin warband trying to bust in!'

Thurston was not amused. 'I don't see why Ben had to let Sniff in the house!' he complained.

'What am I s'posed to do?' I snarled. 'Leave him barking his head off outside the back door? And have Miss Morris round here complaining again? Very smart idea, Thurston!'

'I'm fed up just cutting out Magic Item cards,' grumbled Max. 'Why can't I get on with undercoating the Tiranoc War-chariot?'

'Don't you touch that!' yelled Thurston. 'You can't even stick a coat of arms the right way up on an archer's shield!'

'Right! That's it!' said Max. 'You can stuff your stupid High Elves!' He grabbed a three-pack of Swordmasters and chucked them at Thurston, bouncing them off the top of his head as he ducked.

'God, you're so puerile, Max,' squeaked Thurston, knowing that long words did more damage to Max than any amount of plastic.

'Tell you what, Max,' I said quickly before things got really wiggy. 'You wouldn't like to stick some of that chocolate money under the door, would you? There's a bag of it there, on the mantelpiece. That's it! That should keep Sniff happy for a bit.'

'Can I have some?' said Max, his freckly face unfrowning a bit.

'Course,' I said. 'Anybody else want some?' But the others still hadn't chewed the taste out of the five-fruits flavour Hubba Bubba gum that Bruno had handed round, and shook their heads.

I'd forgotten Max bites his nails and I could see him going cross-eyed trying to open up the seams of the silver paper on the chocolate money. 'Don't bother with that,' I said. 'Sniff'll enjoy the challenge.'

So Max had a good laugh, poking the fat coins one at a time under the door with a ruler, and listening to Sniff's reactions. You could hear him going 'Bbbbrufff?' Then you could hear this skittery sound of claws and silver paper on the polished wooden floor as Sniff played doggy-hockey up and down the hall. Then he did his imitation of a gate on a hinge that needs oiling – 'Mmmeee-eeee-eeee!' – as he twigged there was something to eat inside there. You could imagine his ears popping up straight, his eyes growing wide. Then he went Crunch, Crunch, SCHLOPP – Schlap-Spit-Spit-Spit – and finally he came charging back to the door and huffed through the crack like the big, bad wolf.

It was a toss-up who was having most fun – Sniff or Max – which was just as well, because there had been some heavy bad vibes in our house that morning.

Bad Vibe Number One: Dad had lost the car keys on the day he was supposed to go back to his college to get some special lecture organized for a load of visiting Japanese engineering students. When Mum asked him where the spare keys were, he had to admit he'd already lost the spare keys. So he was pinged up and well cheesed off.

Bad Vibe Number Two: Sal was in wobbly mode and had chucked all her presents down the stairs. She kept screaming 'NOOOOO! Dome want dat wum! I wanna kissmus pwesent!' Apparently nine million teddies, seven hundred and forty thousand stuffed animals, the Duplo farmyard, the Tiny Tears dolly, the Playmobile, the Little Mermaid videos, etc etc didn't count as kissmus presents – so Mum and Dad were feeling dead guilty about giving her a real bummer of a Christmas.

Bad Vibe Number Three: Just to add insult to injury, Mum had had to borrow Bunty's car (a C-reg Metro – so embarrassing!) and drive Dad to work. That meant she had to abandon her plans to spend some time quietly solving the mystery of what exactly Sal meant by 'kissmus pwesent'. Instead, she had to drag Sal with her, kicking and screaming with misunderstood rage. Mum's parting words to me were that if me and the lads made a mess, she would personally run us and the Dragon Princes of Eldor through the food processor.

We had peace for about fifteen minutes. Thurston, Bruno and me got on with the painting, Max fed Sniff under the door, and we all had a chat about what we got for Christmas. Naturally, being so rich, Thurston and Bruno had got the most expensive presents – the Yamaha keyboard, the mountain bike, the 65K electronic organizer, etc, etc.

Still me and Max reckoned we'd done well. Max had got a radio-controlled car and this purple Jungle Stick that went 'Urk Urk' when you scratched your back with it. I'd got a lot of the new software I wanted for my PC, and me and Dad had had a real laugh with my Icky Poo Air Raid – this sticky, glucky yellow thing you could chuck at the wall and it would stick. The only trouble was, Sniff thought it was ace, too. Not only did he keep knocking the pictures down, trying to catch it before it landed, but he got it all covered in spit and dog-hairs, so it soon lost its icky.

Our worst presents were boxer shorts, a colouring-in book and a Transformer video – except for Max, who said his auntie had sent him a 10p piece stuck on a card with sello-tape.

'Wow, would I hate to meet her!' said Bruno, scratching his ear with the pointy end of his paintbrush. 'What is she – a witch or sump'n?'

'Just old,' said Max. He'd fed Sniff the last chocolate sovereign and Sniff had gone all quiet, so Max kept himself busy by lighting a candle and dripping wax on to the back of his hand. 'Yow!' he said. We took no notice, so he kept on torturing himself and going 'Fffff! Agh! Ooo – that hurts! Anybody else want to try it?'

'Oh, well hard, Max!' said Thurston, squinting through his designer gogs while he dabbed yellow paint on the last claw-foot of the Repeating Bolt Thrower. Max was just thinking about dripping some melted wax down the back of Thurston's neck, when Sniff started barking his head off. Mum was back. Soon there was the sound like a spoon being scraped down a window. Sal was back, too, and in a worse temper than when she'd set out, by the sound of it.

We heard the back door open. 'What the . . . ?' yelled Mum. 'Oh, my goodness, the dog's filthy! He's been digging up rubbish again. Who let him in the house? Ben! Ben, where are you? Did you let this dog in?'

Sal stopped screaming for her kissmus pwesent for a sec, so she could tell Sniff off.

'Nuddy boy, Miff!' we heard her say. 'Miff done a big sick on da carpy!'

'RIGHT!' said Mum. 'BENN!!!'

'It's a bwown wum wiv shiny bits in,' explained Sal as Mum's footsteps thundered nearer to the sitting-room.

'Don't open the door, Mum!' I yelled, throwing my weight against it.

'Don't be so ridiculous!' Mum yelled back. 'What's going on in there? she rattled the doorhandle. 'You're not lighting candles, are you?'

'I wanna see in da sitty woom!' screamed Sal.

'Please, Mum! Don't let her in! We've got wet Warhammer Elves all over the floor! She'll ruin them!'

'I wanna wet Wammell!' roared Sal.

'Pleeeez don't let her in, Mum!' I begged. 'We'll do anything.'

'Anything?' said Mum, shushing Sal.

'Anything,' I said.

'Right. You can clear up the dog sick. But first, you can take the tree out and put it by the compost heap.'

'I'll mop up the sick,' I said. 'But don't make me shift the tree, Mum!' I said. 'That's not fair!! Dad promised he'd do something about that. Look, I'll even bath the dog!' I was desperate.

'I know all about your father's promises,' said Mum. 'He also promised to get a spare set of car keys but . . . BAD BOY!!' You could tell that she'd been interrupted by something large and hairy with no manners that shoved her against the hall table and went YIKE!! 'Ben, you fool! What did you want to go mentioning baths for? Now he's hopped it!'

'Oh, no! Was the back door open?' I said.

'What do you think?' said Mum, bitterly. 'I'm really fed up with this family. I shall be jolly glad to see the back of these Christmas holidays!'

That set Sal off about her kissmus pwesent again. Only this time, there was an extra bit . . . 'Wanna go to da shop!'

'What's she on about, Mum?' I yelled

through the key-hole.

'We've just driven past Debenhams,' Mum explained between howls. 'As far as I can make out, she thinks Santa's still hanging about in his Grotto waiting for her to collect her proper Christmas present. She's got the whole Santa business mixed up and she's driving me round the bend! So listen, Ben! I shall take Sal upstairs and she can help me look through all Dad's pockets for the car keys.

Meanwhile, you and your chums can jolly well do your bit and dump the tree! It's been cluttering up the place for far too long!' She rushed up the stairs with Sal, using the old wobble-her-head tactics to try to shake Sal out of her miseries.

I groaned. That tree had been trouble from the start. The bloke at the garden centre said we could have it for twelve quid because it was so big and bushy, most people couldn't handle it. Dad said size was no prob at all, not with our big car.

Have you ever taken part in an attempt to

get in the Guinness Book of Records for the Most Hedgehogs Ever Stuffed into a Passat Estate? That's what it was like driving home with that tree. Well painful! Took us about three hours to get it out, too – because Dad had insisted we load it in tub first, with the point sticking out of the back. Pulling it out was like trying to heave an open umbrella down a chimney. And when we finally dragged the flipping thing clear of the car and stood it up on the drive so that Dad could close the tailgate, Sniff came round the corner and widdled on it. Just to finish off, we had to squeeze this massive, widdly tree through the back door, through the kitchen, along the hall, through the living room door – and over in front of the fireplace. It was like getting vaccinated all over – and that was when the needles were still green!! You could just imagine what it was going to be like if you tried to shift the tree now that the needles were nice and brown and dry and extra sharp!

'Well I'm not touching that tree for a start,'

warned Thurston. 'I've got sensitive skin.'

'And me,' said Max.

Bruno, who's got skin like a rhino, told them not to be such a pair of wimps, squatted down under the tree like a sumo wrestler about to get a grip on the other guy's knickers and ordered me to open one of the bay windows.

'It's miles too big to go through!' I warned, but it was too late. Big Bruno had got a bear hug on the tub, heaved the tree off the carpet, and started staggering towards the daylight. I dashed in front of him, threw one of the windows as wide as I could, and at the same time tried to pull the curtain out of harm's way.

'Go, Brune! Toss that caber!' bawled Max – and BOOM! Bruno and the tree hit the window frame like a couple of linebackers from the Dallas Cowboys American football team. That was OK, but then they shot back into the room as if they'd been hit by a Boeing 707.

Once he heard Bruno yelling, Sniff must

have set off at a gallop from the back garden right round to the front and, when I opened the window, he thought I had something tasty for him in the sitting-room. And when Sniff gets a speed-up, he can't half jump!

Take the BOINNNG-factor from all those springy branches flexing against the wood-work. Add one socking great flying mongrel and you've got Mega-Force!

The tree sort of exploded. Being in that room was like being in the inside of one of those glass snowstorm paper-weights – only with pine needles instead of snow. When Mum charged in with Sal yelling 'Wazzamatta? Wazzappen?', there was a car-pet of pine needles on every surface, includ-ing the heap of bodies piled up in the middle of the floor. Sniff was the top layer. He was spreadeagled in the bare branches of the tree ... which was lying on top of Bruno ... who was flat on his back on top of Max ... who was half-smothering Thurston ... who had sat very painfully on the Repeating Bolt Thrower ... and was squashing the life out of a fair sec-

tion of the High Elf Army. Nobody said a word, not even Thurston, who under other circumstances would have looked for a bit of sympathy. Nobody felt like breathing. Mum folded her arms and took in the whole scene nice and slowly. Her foot started tapping. Not a good sign.

It was Sal who broke the silence. 'Are dey lookin for my kissmuss pwesent under da chwee?'

Nobody moved.

'Well?' said Mum, ice-cold, dead sarcastic. 'Are you?'

We all tried to smile and nod – except Sniff. He took a long look at Sal, rolled his eyes, struggled out of the tree and hopped back out of the window.

'It not dere,' Sal said solemnly. 'Santa got it in da shop.' Her bottom lip came out and her head tipped down. Tears started squirting like a windscreen washer.

Mum didn't give her a chance to get into full waaa-waaa mode. 'I'm sure Sal's Christmas present must be in the house somewhere,' she said, not raising her voice much above a whisper, not opening her teeth more than a millimetre. 'And the boys are going to find it for her while Mummy clears up in here. That's right, isn't it, boys?'

Bruno was the first to stir. He cleared his dry throat. 'Uh . . . sure thang, Missus Moore, Ma'am!' he said.

'Oh, yeah, right,' said Max, getting the idea.

'Absolutely,' said Thurston.

Somehow they all picked themselves up and crept over the pine needle carpet towards the door. Bruno found it a bit tricky to walk, what with the Command Group still drying between his bare toes, but he managed somehow and held out his little finger. 'C'mon, li'l girly,' he said. Sal took hold of it and toddled out into the hall.

Mum looked at the tree, lying there dead among the scattering plastic warriors, the broken lances and battlehorns, the wizards and champions, the banners, the shields . . . 'I shall have to chop it up,' she said, bending down to pick up a brightly painted standard in blue and gold and green. 'Go and get me a saw, Ben, and the secateurs. And about six plastic bin-liners . . . and the Hoover.' She paused to admire the yellow mane and the white battle-rig of the standard bearer's charger, and the neat detail of the blue insignia that Bruno had picked out on the horse's flank. She knelt down among the pine needles to look at other warriors, turning them over slowly and carefully, checking out how smooth they were, noticing the way the excess bits of plastic left after the casting process had been gently rubbed away. 'Hurry up, Ben,' she said. But I could see I didn't have to.

It was Bruno who found the car keys. 'Just a question of getting down to Sal-level,' he explained later. 'Ah told the fellers to just crawl on their bellies and keep an eye out. Wasn't but a couple of minutes before these turned up on a li'l ol' ledge under the kitchen table. Found two golf balls and an egg-cup full of Rice Crispies there, too. Isn't that right, Miss Sal?'

Sal nodded. 'Zigzig's meckmuss,' she said. Only Sal's invisible friend would eat golf balls for breakfast.

'An' I got my kissmus pwesent,' grinned Sal.

'Where on earth did she get those from?' laughed Mum as Sal clumped happily up and down the hall in a filthy old pair of high heels. 'I chucked those out of my wardrobe years ago! I thought Dad had burned them!'

'Santa came from da shop and gib dem to Miff!' said Sal.

Sniff was lying on the kitchen floor, with his head in a mega bowl of trifle out of the fridge. Sal had given it him as a reward for being Santa's messenger.

I thought Mum would go spare – but she was in a hurry to get back into the sitting-room and paint High Elf warriors. She said just to leave the tree and the pine needles and stuff, and not worry about the mess. She thought it was more important to find out from Thurston what colour border she should use to edge a chain mail tunic. 'I think I could really get into this,' she grinned. 'I love this mithrill silver, and this moon yellow makes a fabulous contrast to the deep blue of the cloaks.'

So in spite of interruptions, by lunch time, we were pretty well ready to face Ashley's Goblin ambush. Mum was putting the finishing touches to the jewelled mount on a robe when Max said to her, 'Don't you think it's bad luck, though, Mrs Moore? Having the tree still in the house on the thirteenth day of Christmas, I mean.'

'Well, it's certainly bad luck on Mr Moore,' murmured Mum. 'I shall leave him to clear up this mess when he gets home. Then he can b-a-t-h the d-o-g.'

Clunk, clunk, clunk, went Sal, happy as anything.

SCHLOPP! went Sniff's tongue round the trifle bowl and his tail thumped hopefully. He thought b-a-t-h spelt 'more'.